# TUNNELS OF BLOOD

## THE SAGA OF DARREN SHAN
### BOOK 3

## Other titles by
# DARREN SHAN

## THE SAGA OF DARREN SHAN

## THE DEMONATA

*Also available on audio

# DARREN SHAN

## TUNNELS OF BLOOD

### THE SAGA OF DARREN SHAN
### BOOK 3

HarperCollins *Children's Books*

Madam Octa's on the web… and so is Darren Shan!
For all things freaky, check out the official
Darren Shan website at www.darrenshan.com

First published in Great Britain by HarperCollins *Children's Books* in 2000
This edition published 2009
HarperCollins *Children's Books* is a division of HarperCollins*Publishers* Ltd
77-85 Fulham Palace Road, Hammersmith
London W6 8JB

The HarperCollins website address is:
www.harpercollins.co.uk

1

Text copyright © 2000 Darren Shan

ISBN-13   978 0 00 794551 1

For:

Declan – the original "mr happy"


OBEs (Order of the Bloody Entrails) to:
Jo "the jaguar" Williamson
Zoë "ze zombie" Clarke


The usual monsters:
Liam "Frankenstein" and Biddy "The Bride"
Gillie "rip yer guts out" Russell
the hungry HarperCollins cannibals
and
Emma & Chris – "who ya gonna call?"

# PROLOGUE

THE SMELL of blood is sickening. Hundreds of carcasses hang from silver hooks, stiff, shiny with frosty blood. I know they're just animals — cows, pigs, sheep — but I keep thinking they're human.

I take a careful step forward. Powerful overhead lights mean it's bright as day. I have to tread easily. Hide behind the dead animals. Move slowly. The floor's slippery with water and blood, which makes progress even trickier.

Ahead, I spot him ... the vampire ... Mr Crepsley. He's moving as quietly as I am, eyes focused on the fat man a little way ahead.

The fat man. He's why I'm here in this ice-cold abattoir. He's the human Mr Crepsley intends to kill. He's the man I have to save.

The fat man pauses and checks one of the hanging slabs of meat. His cheeks are chubby and red. He's wearing clear plastic gloves. He pats the dead animal — the squeaky noise of the hook as the carcass swings sets my teeth on edge — then begins whistling. He starts to walk again. Mr Crepsley follows. So do I.

Evra is somewhere far behind. I left him outside. No point

the two of us risking our lives.

I pick up speed, moving slowly closer. Neither knows I'm here. If everything works out as planned, they won't know, not until Mr Crepsley makes his move. Not until I'm forced to act.

The fat man stops again. Bends to examine something. I take a quick step back, afraid he'll spot me but then I see Mr Crepsley closing in. Damn! No time to hide. If this is the moment he's chosen to attack, I have to get nearer.

I sprint forward several metres, risking being heard. Luckily Mr Crepsley is entirely focused on the fat man.

I'm only three or four metres behind the vampire now. I bring up the long butcher's knife which I've been holding down by my side. My eyes are glued to Mr Crepsley. I won't act until he does — I'll give him every chance to prove my terrible suspicions wrong — but the second I see him tensing to spring...

I take a firmer grip on the knife. I've been practising my swipe all day. I know the exact point I want to hit. One quick cut across Mr Crepsley's throat and that'll be that. No more vampire. One more carcass to add to the pile.

Long seconds slip by. I don't dare look to see what the fat man is studying. Is he never going to rise?

Then it happens. The fat man struggles to his feet. Mr Crepsley hisses. He gets ready to lunge. I position the knife and steady my nerves. The fat man's on his feet now. He hears something. Looks up at the ceiling — wrong way, fool! — as Mr Crepsley leaps. As the vampire jumps, so do I, screeching loudly, slashing at him with the knife, determined to kill...

# CHAPTER ONE

*One month earlier...*

MY NAME'S Darren Shan. I'm a half-vampire.

I used to be human, until I stole a vampire's spider. After that, my life changed for ever. Mr Crepsley — the vampire — forced me to become his assistant, and I joined a circus full of weird performers, called the Cirque Du Freak.

Adapting was hard. Drinking blood was harder, and for a long time I wouldn't do it. Eventually I did, to save the memories of a dying friend (vampires can store a person's memories if they drain all their blood). I didn't enjoy it — the following few weeks were horrible, and I was plagued by nightmares — but after that first blood-red drink there could be no going back. I accepted my role as a vampire's assistant and learnt to make the best of it.

Over the course of the next year Mr Crepsley taught me how to hunt and drink without being caught; how to take just enough blood to survive; how to hide my vampire identity when mixing with others. And in time I put my human fears behind me and became a true creature of the night.

*

A couple of girls stood watching Cormac Limbs with serious expressions. He was stretching his arms and legs, rolling his neck around, loosening his muscles. Then, winking at the girls, he put the middle three fingers of his right hand between his teeth and bit them off.

The girls screamed and fled. Cormac chuckled and wriggled the new fingers which were growing out of his hand.

I laughed. You got used to stuff like that when you worked in the Cirque Du Freak. The travelling show was full of remarkable people, freaks of nature with wonderful and sometimes frightening powers.

Apart from Cormac Limbs, the performers included Rhamus Twobellies, capable of eating a full-grown elephant or a tank; Gertha Teeth, who could bite through steel; the Wolf Man, half-man half-wolf, who'd killed my friend Sam Grest; Truska, a beautiful and mysterious woman, who could grow a beard at will; and Mr Tall, who could move as fast as lightning and seemed to be able to read people's minds. Mr Tall owned and managed the Cirque Du Freak.

We were performing in a small town, camped behind an old mill, inside which the show was staged every night. It was a run-down tip, but I was used to such venues. We could have played the grandest theatres in the world and slept in luxurious hotel rooms — the Cirque made a load of money — but it was safer to keep a low profile and stick to places where the police and other officials rarely wandered.

I hadn't changed much since leaving home with Mr Crepsley nearly a year and a half before. Because I was a half-vampire I aged at only a fifth the rate of humans, which meant that though eighteen months had passed, my body was only three or four months older.

Although I wasn't very different on the outside, inside I was an entirely new person. I was stronger than any boy my age, able to run faster, leap further, and dig my extra-strong nails into brick walls. My hearing, eyesight and sense of smell had improved vastly.

Since I wasn't a full-vampire, there was lots of stuff I couldn't do yet. For instance, Mr Crepsley could run at a super-quick speed, which he called flitting. He could breathe out a gas which knocked people unconscious. And he could communicate telepathically with vampires and a few others, such as Mr Tall.

I wouldn't be able to do those things until I became a full-vampire. I didn't lose any sleep over it, because being a half-vampire had its bonuses: I didn't have to drink much human blood and – better yet – I could move about during the day.

It was day when I was exploring a rubbish tip with Evra, the snake-boy, looking for food for the Little People – weird small creatures who wore blue hooded cloaks and never spoke. Nobody – except maybe Mr Tall – knew who or what they were, where they came from, or why they travelled with the Cirque. Their master was a disturbing man called Mr Tiny (he liked to eat *children!*), but we didn't see much of him at the Cirque.

"Found a dead dog," Evra shouted, holding it above his head. "It smells a bit. Do you think they'll mind?"

I sniffed the air – Evra was a long way off, but I could smell the dog from here as well as a human could up close – and shook my head. "It'll be fine," I said. The Little People ate just about anything we brought.

I had a fox and a few rats in my bag. I felt bad about killing the rats – rats are friendly with vampires and usually come up to us like tame pets if we call them – but work is work. We've all got to do things we don't like in life.

There were lots of Little People with the Cirque – twenty of them – and one was hunting with Evra and me. He'd been with the Cirque since soon after me and Mr Crepsley joined. I could tell him apart from the others because he had a limp in his left leg. Evra and me had taken to calling him Lefty.

"Hey, Lefty!" I shouted. "How's it going?" The small figure in the blue hooded cloak didn't answer – he never did – but patted his stomach, which was the sign we needed more food.

"Lefty says to keep going," I told Evra.

"I figured as much," he sighed.

As I prowled for another rat, I spotted a small silver cross in the rubbish. I picked it up and brushed off the dirt. Studying the cross, I smiled. To think I used to believe vampires were terrified of crosses! Most of that stuff in old films and books is hokum. Crosses, holy water, garlic: none of those matter to vampires. We can cross running water. We don't have to be invited into a house before entering. We cast shadows and reflections (though a full-vampire can't be photographed: something to do with bouncing atoms). We can't change shape or fly.

A stake through the heart will kill a vampire. But so will a well-placed bullet, or fire, or a falling heavy object. We're harder to kill than humans but we aren't immortal. Far from it.

I placed the cross on the ground and stood back. Focusing my will, I tried making it jump into my left hand. I stared hard for all of a minute, then clicked the fingers of my right hand.

Nothing happened.

I tried again but still couldn't do it. I'd been trying for months, with no success. Mr Crepsley made it look simple – one click of his fingers and an object would be in his hand, even if it was several metres away – but I hadn't been able to copy him.

I was getting on quite well with Mr Crepsley. He wasn't a

bad old sort. We weren't friends, but I'd accepted him as a teacher and no longer hated him as I had when he first turned me into a half-vampire.

I pocketed the cross, and proceeded with the hunt. After a while I found a half-starved cat in the remains of an old microwave oven. It was after rats as well.

The cat hissed at me and raised its hackles. I pretended to turn my back on it, then spun quickly, grabbed it by the neck and twisted. It gave a strangled little cry and then went limp. I stuck it in the bag and went to see how Evra was doing.

I didn't enjoy killing animals, but hunting was part of my nature. Anyway, I had no sympathy for cats. The blood of cats is poisonous to vampires. Drinking from one wouldn't have killed me but it would have made me sick. And cats are hunters too. The way I saw it, the less cats there were, the more rats there'd be.

That night, back in camp, I tried moving the cross with my mind again. I'd completed my jobs for the day, and the show wouldn't be starting for another few hours, so I'd plenty of time to kill.

It was a cold, late-November night. There hadn't been any snow yet, but it was threatening. I was dressed in my colourful pirate costume: a light green shirt, dark purple trousers, a gold and blue jacket, a red satin cloth round my belly, a brown hat with a feather in it, and soft shoes with toes that curled in on themselves.

I strolled away from the vans and tents and found a secluded spot around the side of the old mill. I stuck the cross on a piece of wood in front of me, took a deep breath, concentrated on the cross and willed it into the palm of my outstretched hand.

No good.

I shuffled closer, so my hand was only centimetres away from the cross.

"I command you to move," I said, clicking my fingers. "I order you to move." Click. "Move." Click. "*Move!*"

I shouted this last word louder than intended and stamped my foot in anger.

"What are you doing?" a familiar voice asked behind me.

Looking up, I saw Mr Crepsley emerging out of the shadows.

"Nothing," I said, trying to hide the cross.

"What is that?" he asked. His eyes missed nothing.

"Just a cross I found while hunting," I said, holding it out.

"What were you doing with it?" Mr Crepsley asked suspiciously.

"Trying to make it move," I said, deciding it was time to ask the vampire about his magic secrets. "How do you do it?"

A smile spread across his face, causing the long scar that ran down the left side to crinkle. "So that is what has been bothering you," he chuckled. He stretched out a hand and clicked his fingers, causing me to blink. Next thing I knew, the cross was in *his* hand.

"How's it done?" I asked. "Can only full-vampires do it?"

"I will demonstrate again. Watch closely this time."

Replacing the cross on the piece of wood, he stood back and clicked his fingers. Once again it disappeared and turned up in his hand. "Did you see?"

"See what?" I was confused.

"One final time," he said. "Try not to blink."

I focused on the small silver piece. I heard his fingers clicking and – keeping my eyes wide open – thought I spotted the slightest blur darting between me and the cross.

When I turned to look at him he was tossing the cross

from hand to hand and smiling. "Rumbled me yet?" he asked.

I frowned. "I thought I saw ... It looked like ..." My face lit up. "You didn't move the cross!" I yelled excitedly. "*You* moved!"

He beamed. "Not as dull as you appear," he complimented me in his usual sarcastic manner.

"Do it again," I said. This time I didn't look at the cross: I watched the vampire. I wasn't able to track his movements — he was too fast — but I caught brief snaps of him as he darted forward, snatched up the cross and leapt back.

"So you're not able to move things with your mind?" I asked.

"Of course not," he laughed.

"Then why the click of the fingers?"

"To distract the eye," he explained.

"Then it's a trick," I said. "It's got nothing to do with being a vampire."

He shrugged. "I could not move so fast if I were human, but yes, it is a trick. I dabbled with illusions before I became a vampire and I like to keep my hand in."

"Could I learn to do it?" I asked.

"Maybe," he said. "You cannot move as fast as I can, but you could get away with it if the object was close to hand. You would have to practise hard — but if you wish, I can teach you."

"I always wanted to be a magician," I said. "But ... hold on..." I remembered a couple of occasions when Mr Crepsley had opened locks with a click of his fingers. "What about locks?" I asked.

"Those are different. You understand what static energy is?" My face was a blank. "Have you ever brushed a comb through your hair and held it up to a thin sheet of paper?"

"Yeah!" I said. "The paper sticks to it."

15

"That is static energy," he explained. "When a vampire flits, a very strong static charge builds up. I have learned to harness that charge. Thus I am able to force open any lock you care to mention."

I thought about that. "And the click of your fingers?" I asked.

"Old habits die hard," he smiled.

"But old vampires die easy!" a voice growled behind us, and before I knew what was happening, someone had reached around the two of us and pressed a pair of razor-sharp knives to the soft flesh of our throats!

# CHAPTER TWO

I FROZE at the touch of the blade and the threatening voice, but Mr Crepsley didn't even blink. He gently pushed the knife away from his throat, then tossed the silver cross to me.

"Gavner, Gavner, Gavner," Mr Crepsley sighed. "I always could hear you coming from half a mile away."

"Not true!" the voice said peevishly, as the blade drew back from my throat. "You couldn't have heard."

"Why not?" Mr Crepsley said. "Nobody in the world breathes as heavily as you. I could pick you out blindfolded in a crowd of thousands."

"One night, Larten," the stranger muttered. "One night I'll catch you out. We'll see how smart you are then."

"Upon that night I shall retire disgracefully," Mr Crepsley chuckled.

Mr Crepsley cocked an eyebrow at me, amused to see I was still stiff and half-afraid, even though I'd figured out our lives weren't in danger.

"Shame on you, Gavner Purl," Mr Crepsley said. "You have frightened the boy."

"Seems all I'm good for," the stranger grunted. "Scaring

children and little old ladies."

Turning slowly, I came face to face with the man called Gavner Purl. He wasn't very tall but he was wide, built like a wrestler. His face was a mass of scars and dark patches, and the rims around his eyes were extremely black. His brown hair was cut short and he was dressed in an ordinary pair of jeans and a baggy white jumper. He had a broad smile and glittering yellow teeth.

It was only when I glanced down at his fingertips and spotted ten scars that I realized he was a vampire. That's how most vampires are created: vampire blood is pumped into them through the soft flesh at the ends of their fingers.

"Darren, this is Gavner Purl," Mr Crepsley introduced us. "An old, trusted, rather clumsy friend. Gavner, this is Darren Shan."

"Pleased to meet you," the vampire said, shaking my hand. "*You* didn't hear me coming, did you?"

"No," I answered honestly.

"There!" he boomed proudly. "See?"

"Congratulations," Mr Crepsley said dryly. "If you are ever called upon to sneak into a nursery, you should have no problems."

Gavner grimaced. "I see time hasn't sweetened you," he noted. "As cutting as ever. How long *has* it been? Fourteen years? Fifteen?"

"Seventeen next February," Mr Crepsley answered promptly.

"Seventeen!" Gavner whistled. "Longer than I thought. Seventeen years and as sour as ever." He nudged me in the ribs. "Does he still complain like a grumpy old woman when he wakes up?" he asked.

"Yes," I giggled.

"I could never get a positive word out of him until midnight. I had to share a coffin with him once for four whole months." He shivered at the memory. "Longest four months of my life."

"You *shared* a coffin?" I asked incredulously.

"Had to," he said. "We were being hunted. We had to stick together. I wouldn't do it again though. I'd rather face the sun and burn."

"You were not the only one with cause for complaint," Mr Crepsley grunted. "Your snoring nearly drove me to face the sun myself." His lips were twitching and I could tell he was having a hard time not smiling.

"Why were you being hunted?" I asked curiously.

"Never mind," Mr Crepsley snapped before Gavner could answer, then glared at his ex-partner.

Gavner pulled a face. "It was nearly sixty years ago, Larten," he said. "I didn't realize it was classified information."

"The boy is not interested in the past," Mr Crepsley said firmly. (I most certainly was!) "You are on *my* soil, Gavner Purl. I would ask you to respect my wishes."

"Stuffy old bat," Gavner grumbled, but gave in with a nod of his head. "So, Darren," he said, "what do you do at the Cirque Du Freak?"

"Odd jobs," I told him. "I fetch food for the Little People and help the performers get ready for—"

"The Little People still travel with the Cirque?" Gavner interrupted.

"More of them than ever," Mr Crepsley answered. "There are twenty with us at the moment."

The vampires shared a knowing glance but said no more about it. I could tell Gavner was troubled by the way his scars knit together into a fierce-looking frown.

"How goes it with the Generals?" Mr Crepsley enquired.

"Usual old routine," Gavner said.

"Gavner is a Vampire General," Mr Crepsley told me. *That* sparked my interest. I'd heard of the Vampire Generals, but nobody had told me exactly who or what they were.

"Excuse me," I said, "but what's a Vampire General? What do they *do*?"

"We keep an eye on rogues like this," Gavner laughed, nudging Mr Crepsley. "We make sure they don't get up to mischief."

"The Vampire Generals monitor the behaviour of the vampire clan," Mr Crepsley added. "They make sure none of us kill innocents or use our powers for evil."

"How do they do that?" I asked.

"If they discover a vampire who has turned bad," Mr Crepsley said, "they kill him."

"Oh." I stared at Gavner Purl. He didn't look like a killer, but then again, there were all those scars...

"It's a boring job most of the time," Gavner said. "I'm more like a village policeman than a soldier. I never did like the term 'Vampire Generals'. Far too pompous."

"It is not just evil vampires that Generals clamp down on," Mr Crepsley said. "It is also their business to crack down on foolish or weak vampires." He sighed. "I have been expecting this visit. Shall we retire to my tent, Gavner, to discuss the matter?"

"You've been *expecting* me?" Gavner looked startled.

"Word was bound to leak out sooner or later," Mr Crepsley said. "I have made no attempt to hide the boy or suppress the truth. Note that please: I will use it during my trial, when I am called upon to defend myself."

"Trial? Truth? The boy?" Gavner was bewildered.

Glancing down at my hands, he spotted the vampire marks on my fingertips and his jaw dropped. "The boy's a *vampire?*" he shrieked.

"Of course." Mr Crepsley frowned. "But surely you knew."

"I knew nothing of the sort!" Gavner protested. He looked into my eyes and concentrated hard. "The blood is weak in him," he mused aloud. "He is only a half-vampire."

"Naturally," Mr Crepsley said. "It is not our custom to make full-vampires of our assistants."

"Nor to make assistants of children!" Gavner Purl snapped, sounding more authoritative than he had before. "What were you thinking?" he asked Mr Crepsley. "A *boy!* When did this happen? Why haven't you informed anybody?"

"It has been nearly a year and a half since I blooded Darren," Mr Crepsley said. "Why I did it is a long story. As for why I have not yet told anyone, that is simpler to answer: you are the first of our kind we have encountered. I would have taken him to the next Council if I had not run into a General beforehand. Now that will not be necessary."

"It bloody well will be!" Gavner snorted.

"Why?" Mr Crepsley asked. "You can judge my actions and pass verdict."

"*Me?* Judge *you?*" Gavner laughed. "No thanks. I'll leave you to the Council. The last thing I need is to get involved in something like this."

"Excuse me," I said again, "but what's this all about? Why are you talking about being judged? And who or what are the Council?"

"I shall tell you later," Mr Crepsley said, waving my questions aside. He studied Gavner curiously. "If you are not here about the boy, why have you come? I thought I made it clear when last we met that I wanted no more to do with the Generals."

"You made it crystal clear," Gavner agreed. "Maybe I'm just here to discuss old times."

Mr Crepsley smiled cynically. "After seventeen years of leaving me to my own devices? I think not, Gavner."

The Vampire General coughed discreetly. "There is trouble brewing. Nothing to do with the Generals," he added quickly. "This is personal. I've come because I feel there's something you should know." He paused.

"Go on," Mr Crepsley urged him.

Gavner looked at me and cleared his throat. "I have no objections to speaking in front of Darren," he said, "but you seemed anxious to steer him clear of certain areas when we were discussing our past a while ago. What I have to tell you may not be for his ears."

"Darren," Mr Crepsley said immediately, "Gavner and I shall continue our discussion in my quarters, alone. Please find Mr Tall and tell him I shall be unable to perform tonight."

I wasn't happy – I wanted to hear what Gavner had to say: he was the first vampire I'd met apart from Mr Crepsley – but from his stern expression, I knew his mind was made up. I turned to leave.

"And Darren," Mr Crepsley called me back. "I know you are curious by nature, but I warn you: do not attempt to eavesdrop. I shall take a dim view of it if you do."

"What do you think I am?" I said. "You treat me like—"

"Darren!" he snapped. "No eavesdropping!"

I nodded glumly. "All right."

"Cheer up," Gavner Purl said as I walked away dejectedly.

"I'll tell you all about it, as soon as Larten's back is turned."

As Mr Crepsley spun round, with fire in his eyes, the Vampire General quickly raised his hands and laughed. "Only joking!"

# CHAPTER THREE

I DECIDED to do the act with Madam Octa — Mr Crepsley's spider — by myself. I was well able to handle her. Besides, it was fun to take over from Mr Crepsley. I'd been on stage with him loads of times, but always as his sidekick.

I went on after Hans Hands — a man who could run a hundred metres on his hands in less than eight seconds — and had great fun. The audience cheered me off, and later I sold loads of candy spiders to clamouring customers.

I hung out with Evra after the show. I told him about Gavner Purl and asked what he knew about Vampire Generals.

"Not much," he said. "I know they exist but I've never met one."

"What about the Council?" I asked.

"I think that's a huge meeting they have every ten or fifteen years," he said. "A big conference where they gather and discuss things."

That was all he could tell me.

A few hours before dawn, while Evra was tending to his snake, Gavner Purl appeared from Mr Crepsley's van — the vampire preferred to sleep in the basements of buildings, but there had been no suitable rooms in the old mill — and asked me to walk with him a while.

The Vampire General walked slowly, rubbing the scars on his face, much as Mr Crepsley often did when thinking.

"Do you enjoy being a half-vampire, Darren?" he asked.

"Not really," I answered honestly. "I've got used to it, but I was happier as a human."

He nodded. "You know that you will age at only a fifth of the human rate? You've resigned yourself to a long childhood? It doesn't bother you?"

"It bothers me," I said. "I used to look forward to growing up. It bugs me that it's going to take so long. But there's nothing I can do about it. I'm stuck, amn't I?"

"Yes," he sighed. "That's the problem with blooding a person: there's no way to take the vampire blood back. It's why we don't blood children: we only want people who know what they're getting into, who wish to abandon their humanity. Larten shouldn't have blooded you. It was a mistake."

"Is that why he was talking about being judged?" I asked.

Gavner nodded. "He'll have to account for his error," he said. "He'll have to convince the Generals and Princes that what he did won't harm them. If he can't..." Gavner looked grim.

"Will he be killed?" I asked softly.

Gavner smiled. "I doubt it. Larten is widely respected. His wrists will be slapped but I don't think anybody will look for his head."

"Why didn't you judge him?" I asked.

"All Generals have the right to pass judgement on non-ranked vampires," he said. "But Larten's an old friend. It's best for a judge to be unbiased. Even if he'd committed a real crime, I would have found it hard to punish him. Besides, Larten's no ordinary vampire. He used to be a General."

"Really?" I stared at Gavner Purl, stunned by the news.

"An important one too," Gavner said. "He was on the verge of being voted a Vampire Prince when he stood down."

"A *prince*?" I asked sceptically. It was hard to imagine Mr Crepsley with a crown and royal cloak.

"That's what we call our leaders," Gavner said. "There are very few of them. Only the noblest and most respected vampires are elected."

"And Mr Crepsley almost became one?" I said. Gavner nodded. "What happened?" I asked. "How did he end up travelling with the Cirque Du Freak?"

"He resigned," Gavner said. "He was a couple of years shy of being invested — we call the process of Prince-making an investiture — when one night he declared he was sick of the business and wanted nothing more to do with the Generals."

"Why?" I asked.

Gavner shrugged. "Nobody knows. Larten never gave much away. Maybe he just got tired of the fighting and killing."

I wanted to ask who it was the Vampire Generals had to fight, but at that moment we cleared the last of the town houses and Gavner Purl smiled and stretched his arms.

"A clear run," he grunted happily.

"You're leaving?" I asked.

"Have to," he said. "A General's schedule is a busy one. I only dropped by because it was on my way. I'd like to stay and chat over old times with Larten, but I can't. Anyway, I think Larten will be on the move soon himself."

My ears perked up. "Where's he going?" I asked.

Gavner shook his head and grinned. "Sorry. He'd scalp me alive if I told. I've already said more than I should. You won't tell him I told you about his being a General, will you?"

"Not if you don't want me to," I said.

"Thanks." Gavner crouched down and faced me. "Larten's a pain in the butt sometimes. He plays his cards too close to his chest, and getting information out of him can be like prying teeth from a shark. But he's a good vampire, one of the best. You couldn't hope for a better teacher. Trust him, Darren, and you won't go wrong."

"I'll try," I smiled.

"This can be a dangerous world for vampires," Gavner said softly. "More dangerous than you know. Stick with Larten and you'll be in a better position to survive than many of our kind. You don't live as long as he has without learning more than your fair share of tricks."

"How old *is* he?" I asked.

"I'm not sure," Gavner said. "I think about a hundred and eighty or two hundred."

"How old are *you*?" I asked.

"I'm a whippersnapper," he said. "Barely past the hundred mark."

"A hundred years old!" I whistled softly.

"That's nothing for a vampire," Gavner said. "I was barely nineteen when first blooded and only twenty-two when I became a full-vampire. I could live to be a good five hundred years old, the gods of the vampires permitting."

"Five hundred...!" I couldn't imagine being so old.

"Picture trying to blow out the candles on *that* cake!" Gavner chuckled. Then he stood. "I must be off. I've fifty kilometres to make before dawn. I'll have to slip into overdrive." He grimaced. "I hate flitting. I always feel sick afterwards."

"Will I see you again?" I asked.

"Probably," he replied. "The world's a small place. I'm sure our paths will cross again one fine gloomy night." He shook my hand. "So long, Darren Shan."

"Until next time, Gavner Purl," I said.

"Next time," he agreed, and then he was off. He took several deep breaths and started to jog. After a while he broke into a sprint. I stood where I was, watching him run, until he hit flitting speed and disappeared in the snapping of an eyelid, at which point I turned and headed back to camp.

I found Mr Crepsley in his van. He was sitting by the window (it was completely covered with strips of dark sticky tape, to block out the sun during the day), staring moodily off into space.

"Gavner's gone," I said.

"Yes," he sighed.

"He didn't stay long," I remarked.

"He is a Vampire General," Mr Crepsley said. "His time is not his own."

"I liked him."

"He is a fine vampire and a good friend," Mr Crepsley agreed.

I cleared my throat. "He said *you* might be leaving too."

Mr Crepsley regarded me suspiciously. "What else did he say?"

"Nothing," I lied quickly. "I asked why he couldn't stay longer and he said there was no point, as you'd probably be moving on soon."

Mr Crepsley nodded. "Gavner brought unpleasant news," he said carefully. "I will have to leave the Cirque for a while."

"Where are you going?" I asked.

"To a city," he responded vaguely.

"What about me?" I asked.

Mr Crepsley scratched his scar thoughtfully. "That is what I have been contemplating," he said. "I would prefer not to take

28

you with me but I think I must. I may have need of you."

"But I like it here," I complained. "I don't want to leave."

"Nor do I," Mr Crepsley snapped. "But I must. And you have to come with me. Remember: we are vampires, not circus performers. The Cirque Du Freak is a means of cover, not our home."

"How long will we be away?" I asked unhappily.

"Days. Weeks. Months. I cannot say for sure."

"What if I refuse to come?"

He studied me ominously. "An assistant who does not obey orders has no purpose," he said quietly. "If I cannot rely on your cooperation, I will have to take steps to remove you from my employ."

"You mean you'd sack me?" I smiled bitterly.

"There is only one way to deal with a rebellious half-vampire," he answered, and I knew what that way was — a stake through the heart!

"It's not fair," I grumbled. "What am I going to do by myself all day in a strange city while you're asleep?"

"What did you do when you were a human?" he asked.

"Things were different," I said. "I had friends and a family. I'm going to be alone again if we leave, like when I first joined up with you."

"It will be hard," Mr Crepsley said compassionately, "but we have no choice. I must be away with the coming of dusk — I would leave now, were we not so near to dawn — and you must come with me. There is no other..."

He stopped as a thought struck him. "Of course," he said slowly, "we could bring another along."

"What do you mean?" I asked.

"We could take Evra with us."

I frowned as I considered it.

"The two of you are good friends, yes?" Mr Crepsley asked.

"Yes," I said, "but I don't know how he'd feel about leaving. And there's his snake: what would we do with that?"

"I am sure somebody could look after the snake," Mr Crepsley said, warming to the idea. "Evra would be good company for you. And he is wiser: he could keep you out of mischief when I am not around."

"I don't need a babysitter!" I huffed.

"No," Mr Crepsley agreed, "but a guardian would not go amiss. You have a habit of getting into trouble when left to your own devices. Remember when you stole Madam Octa? And the mess we had with that human boy, Sam whatever his name was?"

"That wasn't my fault!" I yelled.

"Indeed not," Mr Crepsley said. "But it happened when you were by yourself."

I pulled a face but didn't say anything.

"Will I ask him or not?" Mr Crepsley pressed.

"*I'll* ask him," I said. "You'd probably bully him into going."

"Have it your own way." Mr Crepsley rose. "I will go and clear it with Hibernius." That was Mr Tall's first name. "Be back here before dawn so I can brief you – I want to make sure we are prepared to travel as soon as night falls."

Evra took a lot of time deciding. He didn't like the idea of parting company with his friends in the Cirque Du Freak – or with his snake.

"It won't be for ever," I told him.

"I know," he said uncertainly.

"Look on it as a holiday," I suggested.

"I like the idea of a holiday," he admitted. "But it would be nice to know where I was going."

"Sometimes surprises are more fun," I said.

"And sometimes they aren't," Evra muttered.

"Mr Crepsley will be asleep all day," I reminded him. "We'll be free to do as we like. We can go sightseeing, to cinemas, swimming, whatever we want."

"I've never been swimming," Evra said, and I could tell by the way he grinned that he'd decided to come.

"I'll tell Mr Tall you're coming?" I asked. "And get him to arrange for your snake to be looked after?"

Evra nodded. "She doesn't like the cold weather in any case," he said. "She'll be asleep most of the winter."

"Great!" I beamed. "We'll have a wonderful time."

"We'd better," he said, "or it'll be the last time I come on 'holiday' with you."

I spent the rest of the day packing and unpacking. I only had two small bags to bring, one for me and one for Mr Crepsley, but – apart from my diary, which went everywhere with me – I kept changing my mind about what to put in.

Then I remembered Madam Octa – I wasn't bringing *her* along – and hurried off to find somebody to look after her. Hans Hands agreed to mind her, though he said there was no way he'd let her out of her cage.

Finally, after hours of rushing about – Mr Crepsley had it easy, the wily old goat! – night fell and it was time to leave.

Mr Crepsley checked the bags and nodded curtly. I told him about leaving Madam Octa with Hans Hands and again he nodded. We picked up Evra, said goodbye to Mr Tall and some of the others, then faced away from the camp and began walking.

"Will you be able to carry both of us when you flit?" I asked Mr Crepsley.

"I have no intention of flitting," he said.

"Then how are we going to travel?" I asked.

"Buses and trains," he replied. He laughed when I looked

surprised. "Vampires can use public transport as well as humans. There are no laws against it."

"I suppose not," I said, grinning, wondering what other passengers would think if they knew they were travelling with a vampire, a half-vampire and a snake-boy. "Shall we go, then?" I asked.

"Yes," Mr Crepsley answered simply, and the three of us headed into town to catch the first train out.

# CHAPTER FOUR

IT FELT strange being in a city. The noise and smell nearly drove me mad the first couple of days: with my heightened senses it was like being in the middle of a whirring food blender. I lay in bed during the daytime, covering my head with the thickest pillow I could find. But by the end of the week I'd grown used to the super-sharp sounds and scents and learned to ignore them.

We stayed at a hotel situated in the corner of a quiet city square. In the evenings, when traffic was slow, neighbourhood kids gathered outside for a game of football. I'd have loved to join in but dared not — with my extra strength, I might accidentally end up breaking somebody's bones, or worse.

By the start of our second week we'd fallen into a comfortable routine. Evra and me rose every morning — Mr Crepsley went off by himself at night without telling us where — and ate a big breakfast. After that we'd head out and explore the city, which was big and old and full of interesting stuff. We'd get back to the hotel for nightfall, in case Mr Crepsley wanted us, then watch some TV or play computer games. We usually got to bed between eleven and twelve.

After a year with the Cirque Du Freak, it was a thrill to live like a normal human again. I loved being able to sleep late in the morning, not having to worry about finding food for the Little People; it was great not to be rushing about, running errands for the performers; and sitting back at night, stuffing my face with sweets and pickled onions, watching TV shows – that was heaven!

Evra was enjoying himself too. He'd *never* known a life like this. He'd been part of the circus world for as long as he could remember, first with a nasty side-show owner, then with Mr Tall. He liked the Cirque – I did too – and was looking forward to returning, but he had to admit it was nice to have a break.

"I never realized TV could be so addictive," he said one night, after we'd watched five soap operas in a row.

"My mum and dad never let me watch too much," I told him, "but I knew guys in school who watched five or six hours of it every night of the week!"

"I wouldn't take it that far," Evra mused, "but it's fun in small doses. Perhaps I'll buy a portable set when we return to the Cirque Du Freak."

"I never thought of getting a TV since I joined," I said. "So much else was going on, it was the last thing on my mind. But you're right – it would be nice to have a set, even if only for reruns of *The Simpsons*." That was our favourite show.

I wondered sometimes what Mr Crepsley was up to – he'd always been mysterious, but never *this* secretive – but in truth I wasn't overly bothered: it was nice to have him out of my hair.

Evra had to wrap up in layers of clothes whenever we went out. Not because of the cold – though it *was* chilly: the first snow had fallen a couple of days after our arrival – but because of how he looked. Though he didn't mind people gawping at him – he was used to it – it was easier to get around if he was able to pass for a normal human. That way he didn't have to stop every five or ten minutes to explain to a curious stranger who and what he was.

Covering his body, legs and arms was easy — trousers, a jumper and gloves — but his face was tricky: it wasn't as strongly scaled or coloured as the rest of him, but it wasn't the face of an ordinary human. A thick cap took care of his long yellow-green hair, and dark glasses shaded much of the upper half of his face. But as for the lower half...

We experimented with bandages and flesh-coloured paints before hitting on the answer: a fake beard! We bought it in a joke shop and though it looked silly — nobody could mistake it for a real one — it did the job.

"We must look a right pair," Evra giggled one day as we strolled around a zoo. "You in your pirate costume, me in this get-up. People probably think we're a couple of escaped crazies."

"The folks at the hotel definitely do," I giggled. "I've heard the bellboys and maids talking about us and they reckon Mr Crepsley is a mad doctor and we're two of his patients."

"Yeah?" Evra laughed. "Imagine if they knew the truth — that you're a couple of vampires and I'm a snake-boy!"

"I don't think it would matter," I said. "Mr Crepsley tips well and that's the important thing. 'Money buys privacy', as I heard one of the managers say when a maid was complaining about a guy who'd been walking about naked in the corridors."

"I saw him!" Evra exclaimed. "I thought he'd locked himself out of his room."

"Nope," I smiled. "Apparently he's been walking about starkers for four or five days. According to the manager, he comes every year for a couple of weeks and spends the entire time roaming around, naked as a baby."

"They let him?" Evra asked incredulously.

"'Money buys privacy,'" I repeated.

"And I thought the Cirque Du Freak was a strange place to live," Evra muttered wryly. "Humans are even weirder than us!"

As the days passed the city became more and more Christmassy as people geared themselves up for the twenty-fifth of December. Christmas trees appeared; lights and decorations lit up the streets and windows at night; Father Christmas touched down and took orders; toys of every shape and size filled shop shelves from floor to ceiling.

I was looking forward to Christmas: last year's had passed unnoticed, since Christmas was something hardly anyone associated with the Cirque Du Freak bothered celebrating.

Evra couldn't understand what the fuss was about.

"What's the *point* of it?" he kept asking. "People spend loads of money buying each other presents they don't really need; they drive themselves half-crazy getting a fancy dinner ready; trees and turkeys are bred and slaughtered in frightening numbers. It's ridiculous!"

I tried telling him that it was a day of peace and goodwill, for families to come together and rejoice, but he was having none of it. As far as he was concerned, it was a mad, money-spinning racket.

Mr Crepsley, of course, only snorted whenever the subject was mentioned. "A silly human custom," was how he put it. He wanted nothing to do with the festival.

It would be a lonely Christmas without my family – I missed them more at this time of the year than ever, especially Annie – but I was looking forward to it all the same. The hotel staff were throwing a big party for the guests. There'd be turkey and ham and Christmas pudding and crackers. I was determined to drag Evra into the spirit of the day: I was sure he'd change his opinion when he experienced Christmas first-hand.

"Want to come shopping?" I asked one frosty afternoon, wrapping a scarf around my neck (I didn't need it – my vampire blood kept me warm – nor the thick coat or woolly jumper, but I'd draw attention if I went out without them).

Evra glanced out of the window. It had been snowing earlier and the world outside was frosty-white.

"I can't be bothered," he said. "I don't feel like getting into heavy clothes again." We'd been out that morning, throwing snowballs at each other.

"OK," I said, glad he wasn't coming: I wanted to look over a few presents for him. "I won't be more than an hour or two."

"Will you be back before dark?" Evra asked.

"Maybe," I said.

"You'd better be." He nodded towards the room where Mr Crepsley lay sleeping. "You know how it goes: the one night you aren't here when he wakes will be the one night he wants you."

I laughed. "I'll risk it. Want me to bring you back anything?" Evra shook his head. "OK. See you soon."

I walked through the snow, whistling to myself. I liked snow: it covered up most of the smells and muffled a lot of the noise. Some of the kids who lived in the Square were out building a snowman. I stopped to watch them but moved on before they could ask me to join in: it was easier not to get involved with humans.

As I stood outside a large department store, studying the window display, wondering what to buy Evra, a girl walked over and stood beside me. She was dark-skinned, with long black hair, about my age, and a little shorter than me.

"Ahoy, cap'n," she said, saluting.

"Excuse me?" I replied, startled.

"The costume," she grinned, tugging my coat open. "I think it's cool, you look like a pirate. You going in or just looking?"

"I don't know," I said. "I'm looking for a present for my brother, but I'm not sure what to get him." That was our cover story — that Evra and me were brothers, and Mr Crepsley was our father.

"Right," she nodded. "How old is he?"

"A year older than me," I said.

"Aftershave," she said firmly.

I shook my head. "He hasn't started shaving yet." And never would: hairs wouldn't grow on Evra's scales.

"OK," she said. "How about a CD?"

"He doesn't listen to much music," I said. "Although if I got him a CD player, he might start."

"Those are expensive," the girl said.

"He's my only brother," I said. "He's worth it."

"Then go for it." She held out a hand. She wasn't wearing gloves, despite the cold. "My name's Debbie."

I shook her hand — mine looked very white compared with her dark skin — and told her my name.

"Darren and Debbie." She smiled. "That sounds good, like Bonnie and Clyde."

"Do you always talk like this to strangers?" I asked.

"No," she said. "But we're not strangers."

"We're not?" I frowned.

"I've seen you around," she said. "I live in the Square, a few doors up from the hotel. That's how I knew about the pirate costume. You hang out with that funny guy in glasses and a fake beard."

"Evra. He's the one I'm buying the present for." I tried placing her face but couldn't remember seeing her with the other kids. "I haven't noticed you around," I said.

"I haven't been out much," she replied. "I've been in bed with a cold. That's why I spotted you – I've been spending my days staring out the window, studying the Square. Life gets really boring when you're stuck in bed."

Debbie blew into her hands and rubbed them together.

"You should be wearing gloves," I told her.

"Look who's talking," she sniffed. I'd forgotten to pull on a pair before leaving. "Anyway, that's what I'm here for – I lost my gloves earlier and I've been stomping about from shop to shop trying to find an identical pair. I don't want my parents to find out I lost them on only my second day out of bed."

"What were they like?" I asked.

"Red, with fake fur round the wrists," she said. "My uncle gave them to me a few months ago but didn't say where he got them."

"Have you tried this place yet?" I asked.

"Uh-uh," she said. "I was on my way in when I spotted you."

"Want to come in with me?" I asked.

"Sure," she said. "I hate shopping by myself. I'll help you choose a CD player if you want, I know a lot about them."

"OK," I said, then pushed the door open and held it for her.

"Why, Darren," she laughed, "people will think you fancy me."

I felt myself blushing and tried to think of a suitable response – but couldn't. Debbie giggled, walked in, and left me to trail along behind her.

# CHAPTER FIVE

DEBBIE'S SURNAME was Hemlock and she hated it.

"Imagine being named after a poisonous plant!" she fumed.

"It's not that bad," I said. "I quite like it."

"Shows what sort of taste *you* have," she sniffed.

Debbie had only moved here recently with her parents. She had no brothers or sisters. Her Dad was a computer whiz, who regularly flew around the world on business. They'd swapped homes five times since she was born.

She was interested to learn that I was also used to moving around. I didn't tell her about the Cirque Du Freak but said I was on the road a lot with my dad, who was a travelling salesman.

Debbie wanted to know why she hadn't seen my father in the Square. "I've seen you and your brother loads of times, but never your dad."

"He's an early riser," I lied. "He gets up before dawn and doesn't come back till after dark most days."

"He leaves the two of you alone in the hotel?" She pursed her lips as she considered it. "What about school?" she asked.

"Are these like the gloves you want?" I side stepped the question, picking a pair of red gloves off a rack.

"Nearly," she said, studying them. "Mine were a shade darker."

We went on to another store and looked at loads of CD players. I didn't have much money on me, so I didn't buy anything.

"Of course, after Christmas they'll be reduced in the sales," Debbie sighed, "but what can you do? If you wait, you'll look mean."

"I'm not worried about the money," I said. I could always get some from Mr Crepsley.

After failing to find the right sort of gloves in another couple of shops, we strolled about for a while, watching the lights come on above the streets and in the windows.

"I love this time of evening," Debbie said. "It's as if one city goes to sleep and a new one wakes up."

"A city of night-walkers," I said, thinking of Mr Crepsley.

"Hmmm," she said, looking at me oddly. "Where are you from? I can't place your accent."

"Here and there," I answered vaguely. "Around and about."

"You're not going to tell me, are you?" she asked directly.

"My dad doesn't like me telling people," I said.

"Why not?" she challenged me.

"Can't tell you." I grinned weakly.

"Hmmm," she grunted, but let the matter drop. "What's your hotel like?" she asked. "It looks kind of stuffy. Is it?"

"No," I said. "It's better than most places I've been. The staff don't hassle you if you play in the corridors. And some of the customers..." I told her about the guy who walked about nude.

"No!" she squealed. "You're kidding!"

"Honest," I swore.

"They don't kick him out?"

"He's paying. As far as they're concerned he has the right to walk about however he pleases."

"I'll have to come over sometime," she grinned.

"Whenever you like," I said, smiling. "Except during the day," I added quickly, remembering the slumbering Mr Crepsley. The last thing I wanted was for Debbie to walk in on a vampire while he was sleeping.

We headed back for the Square, taking our time. I liked being with Debbie. I knew I shouldn't be making friends with humans – it was too dangerous – but it was hard to reject her. I hadn't been around anyone my own age, except Evra, since becoming a half-vampire.

"What will you tell your parents about the gloves?" I asked as we stood on the front step of her house.

She shrugged. "The truth. I'll start coughing when I tell them. Hopefully they'll feel sorry for me and won't get too mad."

"Devious," I laughed.

"With a name like Hemlock, are you surprised?" She smiled, then asked, "Do you want to come in for a while?"

I checked my watch. Mr Crepsley would be up and about by now and had probably already left the hotel. I didn't like the idea of leaving Evra alone too long: he might get annoyed if he thought I was neglecting him, and decide to return to the Cirque Du Freak. "Better not," I said. "It's late. I'm expected back."

"Suit yourself," Debbie said. "Feel free to pop over tomorrow if you want. Any time. I'll be in."

"Won't you be at school?" I asked.

She shook her head. "With the holidays so close, Mum said I needn't bother going back until the New Year."

"But she let you out to look for gloves?"

Debbie bit her lip with embarrassment. "She doesn't know I've been out walking," she admitted. "I left in a taxi, telling her I was off to see a friend. I was supposed to come back in a taxi too."

"Ah-ha!" I smiled. "I see the chance for a spot of blackmail."

"Just try it!" she snorted. "I'll cook up a witch's brew and turn you into a frog." She fished a key out of her purse and paused. "You *will* come round, won't you? It gets pretty dull by myself. I haven't made many friends here yet."

"I don't mind coming," I said, "but how will you explain my presence to your mother? You can hardly tell her we met in a taxi."

"You're right." Her eyes narrowed. "I didn't think of that."

"I'm not just a pretty face," I said.

"Not *even* a pretty face!" she laughed. "How about I come over to the hotel?" she suggested. "We can go on to the cinema from there, and I can tell Mum that's where we met."

"OK," I said, and told her my room number. "But not too early," I warned. "Wait until five or six, when it's good and dark."

"OK." She tapped her foot on the doorstep. "*Well?*" she said.

"Well what?" I replied.

"Aren't you going to ask?"

"Ask what?"

"Ask me to go to the cinema," she said.

"But you just—"

"Darren," she sighed. "Girls *never* ask boys out."

"They don't?" I was confused.

"You haven't a clue, have you?" she chuckled. "Just ask me if I want to go to the cinema, OK?"

"OK," I groaned. "Debbie — will you come to the cinema with me?"

"I'll think about it," she said, then unlocked the door and disappeared inside.

*Girls!*

# CHAPTER SIX

EVRA WAS watching TV when I got in. "Any news?" I asked.

"No," he replied.

"Mr Crepsley didn't miss me?"

"He barely noticed you were gone. He's been acting weirdly lately."

"I know," I said. "I'm due a feed of human blood, but he hasn't mentioned it. Normally he's very fussy about making sure I feed on time."

"Are you going to feed without him?" Evra asked.

"Probably. I'll slip into one of the rooms late tonight and take some blood from a sleeping guest. I'll use a syringe." I wasn't able to close cuts with spit like full-vampires could.

I'd come a long way in a year. Not so long ago I'd have jumped at the chance to skip a feed; now I was feeding because I wanted to, not because I'd been told.

"You'd better be careful," Evra warned me. "If you get caught, Mr Crepsley will raise a stink."

"Caught? Me? Impossible! I'll breeze in and out like a ghost."

I did, too, about two in the morning. It was easy for one

with my talents: by sticking an ear to a door and listening for sounds within, I could tell how many people were in a room and whether they were light sleepers or deep sleepers. When I found an unlocked room with a single man snoring like a bear, I let myself in and took the required amount of blood. Back in my own room, I squeezed the blood into a glass and drank.

"That'll keep me going," I said as I finished. "It'll get me through tomorrow anyway, and that's the important thing."

"What's so special about tomorrow?" Evra asked.

I told him about meeting Debbie and arranging to go to the cinema.

"You've got a date!" Evra laughed with delight.

"It's not a date!" I snorted. "We're just going to the cinema."

"*Just?*" Evra grinned. "There's no such thing as *just* with girls. It's a date."

"OK," I said, "it's *kind* of a date. I'm not stupid. I know I can't get involved."

"Why not?" Evra asked.

"Because she's a normal girl and I'm only half-human," I said.

"That needn't stop you going out together. She won't be able to tell you're a vampire, not unless you start biting her neck."

"Ha ha," I laughed dryly. "It's not that. In five years she'll be a grown woman, while I'll still be like this."

Evra shook his head. "Worry about the next five *days*," he advised, "not the next five *years*. You've been hanging around Mr Crepsley too much – you're getting as gloomy as he is. There's no reason for you not to date girls."

"I suppose you're right," I sighed.

"Of course I am."

I chewed my lip nervously. "Assuming it *is* a date," I said, "what do I *do*? I've never been on a date before."

Evra shrugged. "Neither have I. But I guess you just act normal. Chat to her. Tell her a few jokes. Treat her like a friend. Then..."

"*Then...?*" I asked when he stopped.

He puckered up his lips. "Give her a snog!" he chortled.

I threw a pillow at him. "I'm sorry I told you," I grumbled.

"I'm only kidding. But I'll tell you what." He turned serious. "*Don't* tell Mr Crepsley. He'd probably move us on to a new city straightaway, or at least a new hotel."

"You're right," I agreed. "I'll keep quiet about Debbie when he's around. It shouldn't be hard: I barely see him. And when I do, he hardly says anything. He seems to be in a world of his own."

Though I couldn't have known it then, it was a world me and Evra would soon be part of ... and Debbie too.

The next day passed slowly. My belly was a jumble of nerves. I had to drink warm milk to calm it down. Evra didn't help matters. He kept reading the time out loud and commenting: "Five hours to go!" "Four hours to go!" "Three and a half..."

Luckily I didn't have clothes to worry about: I only had the one kind of suit, so there was no problem choosing what to wear. That said, I did spend a couple of hours in the bathroom, checking that I was spotlessly clean.

"Calm down," Evra said eventually. "You look great. I'm half tempted to go out with you myself."

"Shut up, stupid," I snorted, but couldn't help grinning.

"Well, anyway," Evra said, "do you want me to disappear before Debbie arrives?"

"Why?" I asked.

"You might not want me here," he muttered.

"I want to introduce you to her. She thinks you're my brother. It'd look strange if you weren't here when she turns up."

"It's just — well — how will you explain?" Evra asked.

"Explain *what?*"

"My looks," he said, rubbing a few of the scales along his arm.

"Oh," I said, as it finally dawned on me. Debbie didn't know Evra was a snake-boy. She was expecting an ordinary boy.

"I might frighten her," Evra said. "Lots of people get scared when they find themselves face to face with a guy like me. Maybe it would be for the best if—"

"Listen," I said firmly. "You're my best friend, right?"

"Right," Evra smiled weakly. "But—"

"No!" I snapped. "No 'buts'. I like Debbie a lot, but if she can't handle the way you look, too bad."

"Thanks," Evra said quietly.

Night fell and Mr Crepsley arose. The vampire looked haggard. I'd fixed a meal for him — bacon, sausages, pork chops — so he'd eat quickly and leave before Debbie arrived.

"Are you feeling all right?" I asked as he wolfed down the food.

"Fine," he mumbled.

"You look terrible," I told him bluntly. "Have you fed recently?"

He shook his head. "I have not had time. I may tonight."

"I took blood from a guest last night," I said. "It'll keep me going for another week or so."

"Good," he said absentmindedly. It was the first time I'd fed by myself and I'd been expecting some sort of a compliment, but he didn't seem to care. It was like he'd lost interest in me.

I tidied up once he'd left, then sat down to watch TV with Evra and wait for Debbie.

"She's not going to come," I said after what felt like a couple of hours. "She's stood me up."

"Relax," Evra laughed. "You've only been sitting here ten minutes. It's early yet."

I checked my watch – he was right. "I can't go through with this," I groaned. "I've never been out with a girl before. I'll mess it up. She'll think I'm dull."

"Don't get so wound up," Evra said. "You *want* to go out with her and you *are* going out with her, so why worry?"

I started to reply, but was interrupted by Debbie knocking on the door. Forgetting my nerves in an instant, I leapt up to let her in.

# CHAPTER SEVEN

I'D EXPECTED Debbie to dress up, but she was in a pair of jeans and a baggy jumper, wrapped in a long thick coat.

I noticed she was wearing a pair of red gloves.

"You found the gloves?" I asked.

She pulled a face. "They were in my room all along," she groaned. "They'd fallen behind the radiator. Of course, I only found them *after* I'd told Mum about walking about outside without them.

"Are your father and brother here?" she asked.

"Mr Cre— I mean, *Dad's* out. Evra's in." I paused. "There's something you should know about Evra," I said.

"What?"

"He's not like other people."

"Who is?" Debbie laughed.

"You see," I began to explain, "Evra's a—"

"Look," Debbie interrupted, "I don't care what sort of an odd bod he is. Just take me in and make the introductions."

"OK." I grinned shakily and gestured for her to enter. Debbie swished on confidently ahead of me. A couple of steps into the room, she spotted Evra and stopped.

"Wow!" she exclaimed. "Is that a costume?"

Evra smiled nervously. He was standing in front of the telly, arms crossed stiffly.

"Debbie," I said, "this is Evra, my brother. He's—"

"Are those *scales*?" Debbie asked, surging forward.

"Uh-huh," Evra said.

"Can I touch them?" Debbie asked.

"Sure," Evra told her.

She ran her fingers up his left arm — he was wearing a T-shirt — and down his right.

"Wow!" Debbie gasped. "Have you always been like this?"

"Yes," Evra said.

"He's a snake-boy," I explained.

Debbie whirled fiercely on me. "That's a horrible thing to say!" she snapped. "You shouldn't call him names just because he looks different."

"I wasn't calling him—" I began, but she interrupted.

"How would *you* like it if somebody made fun of that stupid costume you wear?" she fumed. I looked down at my suit. "Oh yes!" she snorted. "I could have said plenty about that crazy get-up, but didn't. I figured, if you wanted to look like something out of *The Pirates of Penzance*, that was your choice."

"It's OK," Evra said softly, "I *am* a snake-boy." Debbie stared at Evra uncertainly. "I am, really," he vowed. "I have many serpentine qualities: I shed my skin, I'm cold-blooded, I have snake-like eyes."

"Still," Debbie said, "it's not nice to be compared to a snake."

"It is if you *like* snakes," Evra laughed.

"Oh." Debbie looked back at me, half-ashamed. "Sorry," she said.

"It's OK," I said, secretly pleased that she'd reacted like she had – it proved she wasn't prejudiced.

Debbie was fascinated by Evra and kept asking him questions. What did he eat? How often? Was he able to talk to snakes? After a while I told him to show her his tongue – he had an incredibly long tongue and was able to stick it up his nose.

"That's the grossest, greatest thing I've ever seen!" Debbie howled when Evra demonstrated his nostril-licking abilities. "I wish I could do that. It'd freak the life out of everybody at school."

Eventually it was time to leave for the cinema.

"I won't be late back," I told Evra.

"Don't rush on my account," he said, and winked.

It was a short walk to the cinema and we arrived in plenty of time for the start of the film. We bought popcorn and drinks and headed in. We chatted away to one another during the ads and trailers.

"I like your brother," Debbie said. "He seems a little shy, but I guess that's to do with the way he looks."

"Yes," I agreed. "Life hasn't been easy for him."

"Is anybody else in your family snake-like?" she asked.

"No," I said. "Evra's one of a kind."

"Your mum isn't unusual?" I'd told Debbie my mum and dad were divorced and that Evra and me spent half the year with each. "Or your dad?"

I smiled. "Dad's strange too," I said, "but not like Evra."

"When can I meet him?" she asked.

"Soon," I lied. Debbie had warmed immediately to the snake-boy, but how would she react to a vampire? I'd a feeling she wouldn't take so kindly to Mr Crepsley, not if she knew what he was.

The film was a silly romantic comedy. Debbie laughed more than me.

We discussed the movie afterwards as we walked back to

the Square. I pretended to like it more than I did. As we walked down a dark alley, Debbie took my hand in hers and held on to me for comfort, which made me feel great.

"Aren't you afraid of the dark?" she asked.

"No," I said. The alley seemed quite bright to my vampire-enhanced eyes. "What's to be afraid of?" I asked.

She shivered. "I know it's silly," she said, "but I'm always half-afraid a vampire or werewolf's going to jump out and attack me." She laughed. "Stupid, huh?"

"Yeah," I said, laughing weakly. "Stupid."

If only she knew...

"Your nails are really long," she commented.

"Sorry," I said. My nails were incredibly tough. Scissors couldn't cut them. I had to chew on them with my teeth to keep them down.

"No need to apologize," she said.

As we emerged from the alley, I felt her studying me by the light of the street lamps. "What are you looking at?" I asked.

"There's something different about you, Darren," she mused. "It's not something I can put my finger on."

I shrugged, trying to make light of it. "It's because I'm so good-looking," I joked.

"No," she said seriously. "It's something inside you. I see it in your eyes sometimes."

I looked away. "You're embarrassing me," I grumbled.

She gave my hand a squeeze. "My dad often gives out about that. He says I'm too inquisitive. My mind's always ticking over and I'm forever saying what's on it. I should learn to keep quiet."

We arrived at the Square and I walked Debbie to her door. I stood awkwardly on the front step, wondering what to do next.

Debbie solved the problem for me.

"Want to come in?" she asked.

"Aren't your parents home?" I responded.

"That's OK – they won't mind. I'll tell them you're a friend of a friend."

"Well ... OK," I said. "If you're sure."

"I am," she said, smiling, then took my hand and opened the door.

I was almost as nervous going in as I had been the night I crept down the cellar in the old theatre in my home town, and stole Madam Octa from the sleeping Mr Crepsley!

# CHAPTER EIGHT

AS IT turned out, I had nothing to worry about. Debbie's parents were as nice as she was. Their names were Jesse and Donna – they wouldn't let me call them Mr and Mrs Hemlock – and they made me feel welcome as soon as I walked in.

"Hello!" Jesse said, spotting me first as we entered the living room. "Who's this?"

"Mum, Dad, this is Darren," Debbie said. "He's a friend of Anne's. I ran into him at the cinema and invited him back. Is that OK?"

"Sure," Jesse said.

"Of course," Donna agreed. "We were about to have supper. Would you like some, Darren?"

"If it's no trouble," I said.

"No trouble at all," she beamed. "Do you like scrambled egg?"

"It's my favourite," I told her. It wasn't really, but I guessed it would pay to be polite.

I told Jesse and Donna a bit about myself as we ate.

"What about school?" Jesse asked, as Debbie had before him.

"My dad used to be a teacher," I lied, having given some

thought to the matter since yesterday. "He teaches Evra and me."

"More egg, Darren?" Donna asked.

"Yes please," I said. "It's lovely." It was too. Much nicer than any scrambled egg I'd had before. "What's in it?"

"A few extra spices," Donna said, smiling proudly. "I used to be a chef."

"I wish they had someone like you in the hotel," I sighed. "Their food isn't very good."

I offered to wash the dishes when we were finished but Jesse said he'd do them. "It's my way of unwinding at the end of a hard day," he explained. "Nothing I like better than scrubbing a few dirty dishes, polishing the banisters and Hoovering the carpets."

"Is he kidding?" I asked Debbie.

"Actually, no," she said. "OK if we go up to my room?" she asked.

"Go ahead," Donna told her. "But don't stay nattering too long: we've got a couple of chapters of *The Three Musketeers* to finish, remember?"

Debbie pulled a face. "All for one and one for all," she groaned. "How exciting – I don't think!"

"You don't like *The Three Musketeers*?" I asked.

"Do *you*?"

"Sure. I've seen the movie at least eight times."

"But did you ever read the book?" she asked.

"No, but I read a comic about them once."

Debbie shared a scornful glance with her mother and the two burst out laughing.

"I have to read a bit of a so-called classic every night," Debbie grumbled. "I hope you never learn just how boring those books can be."

"Be down soon," she told her mum, then showed me the way upstairs.

Her room was on the third floor. A big, fairly empty room, with large built-in wardrobes and hardly any posters or ornaments.

"I don't like feeling cluttered," Debbie explained when she saw me looking around.

There was a bare artificial Christmas tree in one corner of the room. There'd been one in the living room too, and I'd noticed a couple more in other rooms on my way up the stairs.

"Why all the trees?" I asked.

"Dad's idea," Debbie said. "He loves Christmas trees, so we get one for every room in the house. The ornaments are in little boxes underneath" — she pointed to a box under the tree — "and we open them on Christmas Eve and decorate the trees. It's a lovely way to pass the night, and it tires you out, so you fall asleep almost as soon as your head hits the pillows."

"It sounds like fun," I agreed wistfully, remembering what it had been like to decorate the Christmas tree at home with my family.

Debbie studied me silently. "You could come over on Christmas Eve," she said. "You and Evra. Your dad too. You could help us with the trees."

I stared at her. "You mean that?"

"Sure. I'd have to check with Mum and Dad first, but I doubt if they'd object. We've had friends over to help before. It's nicer with more people."

I was pleased that she'd asked me, but hesitated before accepting.

"Shall I ask them?" she said.

"I'm not sure if I'll still be here at Christmas. Mr Cre— *Dad* is unpredictable. He goes wherever the job takes him, whenever."

"Well, the offer's there," she said. "If you're here, great. If not"— she shrugged — "we'll manage by ourselves."

We got talking about Christmas presents. "Are you going to get the CD player for Evra?" Debbie asked.

"Yeah. And a few CDs too."

"That just leaves your dad," she said. "What are you getting him?"

I thought about Mr Crepsley and what he might like. I wasn't going to buy him anything — he'd only turn up his nose at presents — but it was interesting to consider what I *could* buy him. What was there that a vampire could possibly be interested in?

I started to smile. "I know," I said. "I'll get him a sun lamp."

"A sun lamp?" Debbie frowned.

"So he can work up a tan." I began to laugh. "He's rather pale. He doesn't get much sun."

Debbie couldn't understand why I was laughing so hard. I'd have liked to let her in on the joke — it would be worth buying the sun lamp just to see the disgusted expression on the vampire's face — but didn't dare.

"You've a weird sense of humour," she muttered, bewildered.

"Trust me," I said, "if you knew my dad, you'd know why I was laughing." I'd tell Evra about my idea when I got home: he'd be able to appreciate it.

We chatted for another hour or so. Then it was time for me to go.

"Well?" Debbie said, as I stood up. "Don't I get a goodnight kiss?"

I thought I was going to collapse.

"I ... um ... I mean ... that is ..." I became a stuttering wreck.

"Don't you want to kiss me?" Debbie asked.

"Yes!" I gasped quickly. "It's just ... I ... um..."

"Hey, forget it," Debbie said, shrugging. "I'm not bothered one way or the other." She got up. "I'll show you out."

We walked quickly down the stairs. I wanted to say goodbye to Jesse and Donna, but Debbie didn't give me the chance. She went straight to the front door and opened it. I was still trying to get back into my coat.

"Can I come round tomorrow?" I asked, struggling to find the left arm of the coat.

"Sure, if you want to," she said.

"Look, Debbie," I said, "I'm sorry I didn't kiss you. I'm just—"

"Scared?" she asked, smiling.

"Yeah," I admitted.

She laughed. "OK," she said. "You can come round tomorrow. I *want* you to. Only next time, be a little braver, OK?" And she closed the door behind me.

# CHAPTER NINE

I LINGERED on the step for ages, feeling stupid. I started back for the hotel but found I was reluctant to return — I didn't want to admit to Evra how dumb I'd been. So I walked around the Square a couple of times, letting the cold night air fill my lungs and clear my head.

I was due to meet Debbie tomorrow, but suddenly felt I couldn't wait that long. My mind made up, I stopped in front of her house and glanced about to make sure I wasn't being watched. I couldn't see anybody, and with my superior eyesight I was sure no one could see me.

I slipped off my shoes and climbed the drainpipe that ran down the front of the house. The window to Debbie's room was three or four metres from the pipe, so when I came level with it, I dug my tough nails into the brick of the building and clawed my way across.

I hung just beneath the window and waited for Debbie to appear.

About twenty minutes later, the light in Debbie's room snapped on. I rapped softly on the glass with my bare knuckles, then rapped again, a little harder. Footsteps approached.

Debbie opened the curtains a notch and stared out, confused. It took her a few seconds to look down and notice me. When she did, she almost collapsed with surprise.

"Open the window," I said, mouthing the words clearly in case she couldn't hear me. Nodding, she dropped to her knees and shoved up the lower pane of glass.

"What are you *doing?*" she hissed. "What are you holding on to?"

"I'm floating on air," I joked.

"You're crazy," Debbie said. "You'll slip and fall."

"I'm perfectly safe," I assured her. "I'm a good climber."

"You must be freezing," she said, spotting my feet. "Where are your shoes? Come in, quick, before you—"

"I don't want to come in," I interrupted. "I climbed up because ... well ... I..." I took a deep breath. "Is the offer still on?"

"What offer?" Debbie asked.

"The offer of a kiss," I said.

Debbie blinked, then smiled. "You *are* mad," she chuckled.

"One hundred per cent crazy," I agreed.

"You went to all this trouble just for that?" she asked.

I nodded.

"You could have knocked on the door," she said.

"I didn't think of that," I smiled. "So — how about it?"

"I suppose you deserve one," she said, "but quickly, OK?"

"All right," I agreed.

Debbie stuck her head out. I leaned forward, heart beating, and pecked her lips.

She smiled. "Worth coming up for?" she asked.

"Yes," I said. I was shaking, and it wasn't from the cold.

"Here," she said. "Here's another one."

She kissed me sweetly and I almost lost my grip on the wall.

When she moved away, she was smiling mysteriously. I could feel myself grinning like an idiot.

"See you tomorrow, Romeo," she said.

"Tomorrow," I sighed happily.

As the window shut and the curtains closed, I climbed down, delighted with myself. I practically bounced back to the hotel. I was almost at the door before I remembered my shoes. Dashing back, I retrieved them, shook the snow off and stuck them on.

By the time I got to the hotel, I'd regained my composure. I opened the door of my room and entered. Evra was watching TV. He was focused on the screen and barely noticed me coming in.

"I'm back," I said, taking off my coat. He didn't reply. "I'm back!" I repeated, louder.

"Um," he grunted, waving distractedly at me.

"That's a fine attitude," I sniffed. "I thought you'd be interested in how the evening went. I'll know better next time. In future, I'll just—"

"Have you seen the news?" Evra asked quietly.

"It may surprise you to learn, young Evra Von," I said sarcastically, "that they don't show news reels in cinemas any longer. Now, do you want to hear about my date or not?"

"You should watch this," Evra said.

"Watch *what*?" I asked, irritated. I walked around behind him and saw it was a news programme. "The *news*?" I laughed. "Turn it off, Evra, and I'll tell you about—"

"Darren!" Evra snapped in a most unusual tone. He looked up at me and his face was a mask of worry. "You should watch this," he said again, slowly this time, and I realized he wasn't fooling.

Sitting down, I studied the screen. There was a picture of the outside of a building on it, then the camera dissolved to an interior shot and scanned round the walls. A caption informed viewers that the photographs were from stock footage, which meant they'd been filmed sometime in the past. A reporter was waffling on about the building.

"What's the big deal?" I asked.

"This is where they found the bodies," Evra said softly.

"What bodies?"

"Watch," he said.

The camera came to rest in a dark room that looked the same as all the others, held on the scene for a few seconds, then dissolved back to a view of the building's exterior. The caption informed us that these new pictures had been shot earlier today. As I watched, several policemen and doctors emerged from the building, pushing mobile stretchers, each of which held a motionless object covered by a body bag.

"Are those what I think they are?" I asked quietly.

"Corpses," Evra confirmed. "Six so far. The police are still searching the building."

"What does it have to do with *us*?" I asked uneasily.

"Listen." He turned up the sound.

A reporter was talking into the camera now, live, explaining how the police found the bodies — a couple of teenagers had stumbled over them while exploring the deserted building as a dare — and when, and how the search was progressing. The reporter looked rather stunned.

The newsreader in the studio asked the reporter a question about the bodies, to which she shook her head.

"No," she said, "the police aren't issuing names, and won't until the relatives of the deceased have been notified."

"Have you learned any more about the nature of their

deaths?" the newsreader asked.

"No," the reporter replied. "The police have blocked the flow of information. We've only the early reports to go on. The six people — we don't know if they're men or women — appear to be victims of a serial killer or some sort of sacrificial cult. We don't know about the last two bodies brought up, but the initial four all shared the same bizarre wounds and conditions."

"Could you explain once again what those conditions were?" the newsreader asked.

The reporter nodded. "The victims — at least the first four — have slit throats, which seem to be the means by which they were killed. In addition, the bodies appear — and I must stress that this is an early, unverified report — to have been drained of all their blood."

"Possibly sucked out or pumped dry?" the newsreader suggested.

The reporter shrugged. "As of the moment, nobody can answer that, except the police." She paused. "And, of course, the murderer."

Evra switched the sound off but left the picture on.

"See?" he said softly.

"Oh no," I gasped. I thought of Mr Crepsley, who'd been out alone every night since we arrived, prowling the city for reasons he wouldn't reveal. I thought of the six bodies and the reporter's and newsreader's comments: "...drained of all their blood." "Possibly sucked out or pumped dry."

"Mr Crepsley," I said. And for a long time I gazed in silence at the screen, unable to say anything more.

# CHAPTER TEN

I PACED furiously around the hotel room, hands clenched into fists, cursing angrily, Evra watching mutely.

"I'm going to kill him," I finally muttered. "I'll wait for day, pull back the curtains, drive a stake through his heart, chop his head off, and set him on fire."

"You don't believe in taking chances, do you?" Evra remarked wryly. "I suppose you'll scoop his brains out too and stuff the space inside his head with garlic."

"How can you make jokes at a time like this?" I howled.

Evra hesitated. "It mightn't have been him."

"Come off it!" I barked. "Who else could it have been?"

"I don't know."

"The blood was sucked out of them!" I shouted.

"That's what the reporters *think*," Evra said. "They weren't certain."

"Maybe we should wait," I huffed. "Wait for him to kill another five or six, huh?"

Evra sighed. "I don't know what we should do," he said. "But I think we should have proof before we go after him. Chopping a person's head off is kind of final. If we find out later we were mistaken, there's no going back. We can't glue his head back on and say, 'Sorry, all a big mistake, no hard feelings'."

He was right. Killing Mr Crepsley without proof would be wrong. But it had to be him! Those nights out, acting so strangely, not telling us what he was doing — it all added up.

"There's something else," Evra said. I glanced down at him. "Let's say Mr Crepsley *is* the killer."

"I've no problem accepting that," I grunted.

"Why would he do it?" Evra asked. "It's not his style. I've known him longer than you have, and I've never seen or heard of him doing anything like this. He's not a killer."

"He probably killed when he was a Vampire General," I said. I'd told Evra about my conversation with Gavner Purl.

"Yes," Evra agreed. "He killed evil vampires, who deserved to be killed. What I'm saying is, if he did kill these six people, maybe *they* had to be killed too. Maybe they were vampires."

I shook my head. "He gave up being a Vampire General years ago."

"Gavner Purl could have persuaded him to join again," Evra said. "We don't know anything about the Vampire Generals or how they work. Perhaps that's why Mr Crepsley came here."

It sounded halfway reasonable, but I didn't believe it.

"Six evil vampires on the loose in one city?" I asked. "What are the odds against that?"

"Who knows?" Evra said. "Do *you* know how an evil vampire behaves? *I* don't. Maybe they form gangs."

"And Mr Crepsley wiped them out by himself?" I said. "Vampires are tough to kill. He'd have no problem killing six humans, but six vampires? No way."

"Who says he was alone?" Evra asked. "Maybe Gavner

Purl was with him. Maybe there's a load of Vampire Generals in town."

"Your argument's getting weaker by the second," I commented.

"Possibly," Evra said, "but that doesn't mean I'm wrong. *We don't know*, Darren. You can't kill Mr Crepsley on a hunch. We have to wait. Think about it and you'll see I'm right."

I calmed down and thought it over. "OK," I sighed. "He's innocent till proven guilty. But what should we do? Sit back and pretend nothing's happened? Report him to the police? Ask him straight to his face?"

"If we were at the Cirque Du Freak," Evra mused, "we could tell Mr Tall and leave it in his hands."

"But we're not at the Cirque," I reminded him.

"No," he said. "We're on our own." His narrow eyes narrowed even further as he mulled it over. "How about this? We track him every night when he leaves, see where he goes and what he gets up to. If we find out he's the killer, and that these are ordinary humans, then we kill him."

"You'd do that?" I asked.

Evra nodded. "I've never killed before," he said quietly, "and I hate the thought of it. But if Mr Crepsley is murdering without good cause, I'll help you kill him. I'd rather leave it to someone else, but since there isn't anybody..."

His face was set and I knew I could rely on him.

"But we have to be *sure*," Evra warned me. "If there's even a glimmer of doubt, we mustn't do it."

"Agreed," I said.

"And it has to be a joint decision," Evra added. "You have to promise you won't kill him without my approval."

"OK."

"I'm serious," he told me. "If I think Mr Crepsley is

67

innocent, and you go after him, I'll do everything I can to stop you. Even if it means..." He left the threat unfinished.

"Don't worry," I said. "This isn't something I'm looking forward to. I've grown used to Mr Crepsley. The last thing I want to do is kill him."

I was telling the truth. I'd love it if my suspicions turned out to be unwarranted. But I had an awful feeling they wouldn't.

"I hope we're wrong about this," Evra said. "Saying we'll kill him is easy, but doing it would be a lot harder. He's not the sort to lie there and do nothing while under attack."

"We'll worry about that later," I said. "For the moment, let's turn the sound back up. If we're lucky, the police will solve the case and it'll be nothing more than a crazy human who's seen one too many Dracula films."

I sat down beside Evra and we spent the rest of night watching the news, rarely speaking, waiting for the vampire — the *killer?* — to return.

# CHAPTER ELEVEN

SHADOWING MR Crepsley wasn't easy. The first night we lost him after a couple of minutes: he shot up a fire escape and by the time we got to the top he was nowhere to be seen. We wandered around the city for a few hours, hoping to chance upon him, but saw neither hide nor hair of him for the rest of the night.

We learned from that experience. While Mr Crepsley slept the next day, I went and bought a pair of mobile phones. Evra and me tested them out before dusk and they worked pretty well.

That night, when Mr Crepsley took to the rooftops, Evra stuck to the ground. He couldn't move as fast as me. By myself, I was able to keep track of the vampire and pass the information on to Evra, who followed on the ground.

Even alone, it was difficult to keep up. Mr Crepsley could move a lot quicker than me. Fortunately, he had no idea I was after him, so he didn't go as fast as he could, since he didn't think he'd any need to.

I kept him in sight for three hours that night, before losing him when he slipped down to street level and took a couple of turns that I missed. The next night I stuck with him until dawn. It varied after that: some nights I'd lose him within an hour; others I'd be on his tail till morning.

He didn't do much while I was following him. Sometimes he'd stop in one place for ages, above crowds of people, and observe them silently (picking out his next victim?). Other times he roamed without pause. His routes were unpredictable: he might go the same way two or three nights in a row, or try entirely new directions every night. It was impossible to second-guess him.

Evra was exhausted at the end of each night — I kept forgetting he wasn't as powerful as me — but he never complained. I said he could stay in a few nights if he wanted, but he shook his head and insisted on coming with me.

Maybe he thought I'd kill Mr Crepsley if he wasn't around.

Maybe he was *right*.

No fresh bodies had been discovered since news of the six in the building broke. It had been confirmed that all the bodies had been drained of their blood, and that they were ordinary humans: two men and four women. All were young — the oldest was twenty-seven — and from different parts of the city.

Evra's disappointment was evident when he heard the victims were normal people — it would have made life much easier if they'd been vampires.

"Would doctors be able to tell the difference between a human and a vampire?" he asked.

"Of course," I replied.

"How?"

"Different sort of blood," I said.

"But they were drained of blood," he reminded me.

"Their cells wouldn't be the same. Atoms act strangely in vampires — that's why they can't be photographed. And they'd have extra tough nails and teeth. The doctors would know, Evra."

I was trying to keep an open mind. Mr Crepsley hadn't killed anyone while we'd been following him, which was a hopeful sign. On the other hand, maybe he was waiting for the fuss to die down before striking again — at the moment, if somebody was late home from school or work, alarm bells rang immediately.

Or perhaps he *had* killed. Maybe he knew we were following him and was only killing when he was certain he'd lost us. That was unlikely, but I didn't rule it out completely. Mr Crepsley could be cunning when he wanted. I wouldn't have put anything past him.

Though I was sleeping through most of the days — in order to stay awake at night — I made a point of waking a couple of hours before sunset to spend some time with Debbie. Usually I went over to her house and we sat upstairs in her bedroom and played music and talked — I was always looking to conserve energy for the night chase ahead — but sometimes we'd go for a walk or hit the shops.

I was determined not to let Mr Crepsley ruin my friendship with Debbie. I loved being with her. She was my first girlfriend. I knew we'd have to part sooner rather than later — I hadn't forgotten what I was — but I wouldn't do anything to shorten our time together. I'd given up my nights to pursue Mr Crepsley. I wasn't going to give up my days too.

"How come you don't come round after dark any more?" she asked one Saturday as we emerged from a cinema matinée. I'd risen earlier than usual, in order to spend the day with her.

"I'm afraid of the dark," I whimpered.

"Seriously," she said, pinching my arm.

"My dad doesn't like me going out at night," I lied. "He feels a bit guilty, not being around during the day. He likes Evra and me to sit with him at night and tell him what we've been up to."

"Surely he wouldn't mind if you went out now and then," Debbie protested. "He let you out the night of our first date, didn't he?"

I shook my head. "I sneaked out," I said. "He went mad when he found out. Wouldn't talk to me for a week. That's why I haven't taken you round to meet him – he's still fuming."

"He sounds like a right old misery-guts," Debbie said.

"He is," I sighed. "But what can I do? He's my dad. I have to stick by him."

I felt bad lying to her, but I could hardly tell her the truth. I smiled to myself when I imagined breaking the news: "That guy I say is my father? He's not. He's a vampire. Oh, and I think he's the one who killed those six people."

"What are you smiling at?" Debbie asked.

"Nothing," I said quickly, wiping the smile from my face.

It was a strange double life – normal boy by day, deadly vampire-tracker by night – but I was enjoying it. If it had been a year or so earlier, I'd have been confused; I'd have tossed and turned in my sleep, worrying about what the next night would bring; my eating habits might have been affected and I'd have become depressed; I'd probably have chosen to focus on one thing at a time, and stopped meeting Debbie.

Not now. My experiences with Mr Crepsley and the Cirque Du Freak had changed me. I was able to handle two different roles. In fact, I liked the variation: tracking the vampire at night made me feel big and important – Darren

Shan, protector of the sleeping city! — and seeing Debbie in the afternoons let me feel like a normal human boy. I had the best of both worlds.

That stopped when Mr Crepsley zoomed in on the next victim — the fat man.

# CHAPTER TWELVE

I DIDN'T realize at first that Mr Crepsley was following someone. He was hovering above a busy shopping street, where he'd been for the better part of an hour, studying the shoppers. Then, without warning, he climbed to the top of the building he'd been clinging to and started across the roof.

I rang Evra. He never rang me, for fear the vampire would hear my phone. "He's on the move again," I said quietly.

"About time," Evra grumbled. "I hate it when he stops. You don't know how cold it gets, standing still down here."

"Go get something to eat," I told him. "He's moving pretty slowly. I think you can take five or ten minutes off."

"Are you sure?" Evra asked.

"Yes," I said. "I'll ring you if anything happens."

"OK," Evra said. "I fancy a hot dog and a cup of coffee. You want me to pick something up for you?"

"No thanks," I said. "I'll keep in touch. See you soon." I hit the off switch and started after the vampire.

I didn't like eating stuff like hot dogs, burgers or French fries while tracking Mr Crepsley: his nose could easily detect such strong scents. I ate dry slices of bread – which produced almost no smell – to keep hunger at bay. I had ordinary tap water in a bottle to drink.

After several minutes I grew curious. The other nights, he'd either kept to one spot or wandered about without direction. He was moving with purpose this time.

I decided to get closer. It was dangerous, especially since he wasn't rushing – he was more likely to spot me – but I had to see what he was up to.

Closing the gap by a third – as near to him as I dared get – I saw that he was sticking his head out over the edge of the roof, keeping a watch on the street below.

Glancing down at the well-lit street, I couldn't spot who he was after. It was only when he paused above a lamp that I noticed the fat man at the base, adjusting his laces.

That was it! Mr Crepsley was after the fat man! I knew by the way the vampire stared, waiting for him to tie his laces and move on. When the fat man did eventually stand and start walking again, sure enough, Mr Crepsley followed.

Taking a few steps back, I rang Evra.

"What's up?" he asked. I could hear him munching on his hot dog. There were voices in the background.

"Action," I said simply.

"Oh hell!" Evra gasped. I heard him dropping the hot dog and shuffling away from the people behind him, to a quieter spot. "Are you sure?" he asked.

"Positive," I said. "Quarry has been sighted."

"OK," Evra sighed. He sounded nervous. I didn't blame him – I was nervous too. "OK," he said again. "Give me your position."

I read out the name of the street. "But don't rush," I told him. "They're moving slowly. Stay a couple of streets back. I don't want Mr Crepsley spotting you."

"*I* don't want him spotting me either!" Evra snorted. "Keep me up to date."

"Will do," I promised. Switching off, I started after the pursuing vampire.

He trailed the fat man to a large building, which the human disappeared into. Mr Crepsley waited half an hour, then slowly circled the building, checking on windows and doors. I trudged along behind, keeping my distance, ready to race after him if he entered.

He didn't. Instead, when he was through examining the place, he retired to a nearby rooftop, from where he had a perfect view of all the entrances, and sat down to wait.

I told Evra what was happening.

"He's just sitting there?" Evra asked.

"Sitting and watching," I confirmed.

"What sort of a place is it?"

I'd read the name on the walls while I was passing, and seen in a couple of the windows, but I could have told Evra what went on in the building simply by the foul smell of animal blood in the air.

"It's an abattoir," I whispered.

There was a long pause. Then: "Maybe he's just here for the animal blood," Evra suggested.

"No. He would have entered by now if that was the case. He didn't come for the animals. He came here for the human."

"We don't *know* that," Evra said. "Maybe he's waiting for it to close before going in."

"He'd have a long wait," I laughed. "It stays open all night."

"I'm coming up," Evra said. "Don't move until I get there."

"I'll move when Mr Crepsley moves, whether you're here or not," I said, but Evra had switched off and didn't hear me.

He arrived a few minutes later, his breath stinking of

mustard and onions. "Dry bread for you from now on," I muttered.

"Do you think Mr Crepsley will smell me?" Evra asked. "Maybe I should go back down and—"

I shook my head. "He's too close to the abattoir," I said. "The smell of blood will block everything else out."

"Where is he?" Evra asked. I pointed the vampire out. Evra had to squint, but eventually spotted him.

"We have to be extra quiet," I said. "Even a slight noise could have him swooping down on us."

Evra shivered — whether because of the cold, or the thought of being attacked, I don't know — and settled down. We said little to each other after that.

We had to breathe into our cupped fists to stop our breath from showing. We'd have been all right if it had been snowing — the snow would have hidden the smoke-like tendrils — but it was a clear and frosty night.

We sat there until three in the morning. Evra's teeth were chattering, and I was on the point of sending him home before he froze to death, when the fat man emerged. Mr Crepsley started after him immediately.

Too late, I realized the vampire was going to pass by us on his way back. There was no time to hide. He'd see us!

"Keep perfectly still," I whispered to Evra. "Don't even breathe."

The vampire came towards us, walking steadily across the icy roofs in his bare feet. I was certain he'd spot us, but his eyes were trained on the human. He passed within five metres of us — his shadow crept over me like some awful ghost — and then he was gone.

"I think my heart's stopped," Evra said shakily.

I heard the familiar thump-thump sounds of the snake-boy's heart (it beat slightly slower than a normal human's) and smiled. "You're OK," I told him.

"I thought we were done for," Evra hissed.

"Me too." I stood and checked which way the vampire was going. "You'd better slip back down to the street," I told Evra.

"He's not going fast," Evra said. "I can keep up."

I shook my head. "There's no telling when he'll speed up: the man might get in a cab or have a lift waiting. Besides, after our narrow escape, it's better we split: that way, if one of us gets caught, the other can sneak back to the hotel and pretend he wasn't involved."

Evra saw the sense in that and clambered down the nearest fire escape. I began dogging the tracks of the vampire and the fat man.

He walked back the way he'd come, past the deserted street where we'd first picked him up, on to a block of flats.

He lived in one of the central flats on the sixth floor. Mr Crepsley waited for the lights to go off inside, then went up in the lift. I ran up the stairs and watched from the far end of the landing.

I expected him to open the door and enter – locks were no problem for the vampire – but all he did was check the door and windows. Then he turned around and went back to the lift.

I hurried down the stairs and tagged the vampire as he strolled away from the flats. I told Evra what had happened and where the vampire was heading. A few minutes later he joined up with me and we followed Mr Crepsley as he jogged through the streets.

"Why didn't he go in?" Evra asked.

"I don't know," I said. "Maybe there was somebody else there. Or maybe he plans to come back later. One thing's for sure: he didn't go up there to post a letter!"

After a while, we rounded a corner into an alley and spotted Mr Crepsley bent over a motionless woman. Evra gasped and started forward. I caught his arm and yanked him back.

"*What are you doing?*" he hissed. "Didn't you see? He's attacking! We have to stop him before—"

"It's OK," I said. "He isn't attacking. He's feeding."

Evra's struggles ceased. "You're sure?" he asked suspiciously.

I nodded. "He's drinking from the woman's arm. The corpses in the building had their throats cut, remember?"

Evra nodded uncertainly. "If you're wrong..."

"I'm not," I assured him.

Minutes later, the vampire moved on, leaving the woman behind. We hurried down the alley to check. As I'd guessed, she was unconscious but alive, a small fresh scar on her left arm the only sign that she had been feasted upon.

"Let's go," I said, standing. "She'll wake in a few minutes. We'd better not be here when she does."

"What about Mr Crepsley?" Evra asked.

I looked up at the sky, gauging how long was left until dawn. "He won't kill anyone tonight," I said. "It's too late. He's probably heading back for the hotel. Come on – if we don't get back before him, we'll have a hell of a time trying to explain where we were."

# CHAPTER THIRTEEN

BEFORE DUSK descended the next night, Evra went round to the block of flats to keep watch on the fat man. I stayed home, in order to follow Mr Crepsley. If the vampire headed for the flats, I'd join Evra. If he went elsewhere, we'd discuss the situation and decide whether Evra should desert his post or stay.

The vampire rose promptly as the sun went down. He was looking more cheerful tonight, though he still wouldn't have appeared out of place in a funeral parlour.

"Where is Evra?" he asked, tucking into the meal I'd prepared.

"Shopping," I said.

"By himself?" Mr Crepsley paused. For a moment I thought he was suspicious, but he was just looking for the salt.

"I think he's buying Christmas presents," I said.

"I thought Evra was above such absurdities. What is the date, anyway?"

"The twentieth of December," I answered.

"And Christmas is the twenty-fifth?"

"Yes," I said.

Mr Crepsley rubbed his scar thoughtfully. "My business here may have come to an end by then," he said.

"Oh?" I tried not to sound curious or excited.

"I had planned to move on as soon as possible, but if you wish to remain here for Christmas, we can. I understand the staff are hosting some kind of celebration?"

"Yes," I said.

"You would like to attend?"

"Yes." I forced a smile. "Evra and me are buying presents for each other. We're going to eat dinner with the rest of the guests and pull crackers and stuff ourselves with turkey. You can take part too, if you want." I tried to make it sound like I wanted him there.

He smiled and shook his head. "Such follies do not appeal to me," he said.

"Suit yourself," I replied.

As soon as he left, I started after him. He led me straight to the abattoir, which surprised me. Maybe it wasn't the fat man he was interested in: perhaps there was something – or somebody – else here that he had his eye on.

I discussed it with Evra over the phone.

"It's curious," he agreed. "Maybe he wants to catch him when he's entering or leaving work."

"Maybe," I said uncertainly. Something seemed odd about it. The vampire wasn't behaving as I'd expected him to.

Evra stayed where he was, to follow the fat man. I chose a safe spot to hide, next to a warm pipe that kept some of the cold out. My view of the abattoir wasn't as good as it had been last night, but I had a clear sight of Mr Crepsley, which was what mattered.

The fat man arrived at the scheduled time, Evra soon after him. I moved to the edge of the roof when I saw them, ready to leap down and intervene if Mr Crepsley made his move. But the vampire remained stationary.

And that was it for the night. Mr Crepsley sat on his ledge; Evra and me crouched on ours; the workers kept the abattoir ticking over. At three in the morning, the fat man re-appeared and went home. Once again Mr Crepsley followed and once again we followed Mr Crepsley. This time the vampire didn't go up to the landing, but that was the only variation in the routine.

The next night, the exact same thing happened.

"What's he up to?" Evra asked. The cold was getting to him and he was complaining about cramps in his legs. I'd told him he could leave but he was determined to stick it out.

"I don't know," I said. "Perhaps he's waiting for a special time to act. Maybe the moon has to be in a certain position or something."

"I thought werewolves were the only monsters affected by the moon," Evra said, half-jokingly.

"I thought so too," I said. "But I'm not sure. There's so much Mr Crepsley hasn't told me about being a full-vampire. You could fill a book with all the stuff I know nothing about."

"What are we going to do if he attacks?" Evra asked. "Do you think we stand a chance against him in a fight?"

"Not a fair fight," I said. "But in a dirty one..." I pulled out a long rusty butcher's knife, let Evra's eyes focus on it, then slipped it back beneath my shirt.

"Where did you get that?" Evra gasped.

"I came sniffing round the abattoir today, to familiarize myself with the layout, and found this knife lying in a bin out back. I guess it was too rusty to be of any use."

"That's what you're going to use?" Evra asked quietly.

I nodded. "I'll slit his throat," I whispered. "I'll wait for him to make his move, then..." I clenched my jaw shut.

"You reckon you can do it? He's really fast. If you miss your first chance, you're unlikely to get a second."

"He won't be expecting me," I said. "I can do it." I faced Evra. "I know we agreed to do this together, but I want to go after him by myself when the time comes."

"No way!" Evra hissed.

"I have to," I said. "You can't move as quietly or as quickly as me. If you come, you'll be in the way. Besides," I added, "if things go badly and I fail, you'll still be around to take another shot at him. Wait for day and get him while he's sleeping."

"Maybe that's the best solution," Evra said. "Maybe we should *both* wait. The main reason we're here is to confirm he's the killer. If he is, and we get proof, why don't we wait and—"

"No," I said softly. "I won't let him murder that man."

"You know nothing about him," Evra said. "Remember what I suggested: that the six dead people may have been killed because they were evil? Perhaps this guy's rotten."

"I don't care," I said stubbornly. "I only agreed to go along with Mr Crepsley because he convinced me he wasn't bad, that he didn't kill people. If he is a killer, I'm guilty too, for believing him and helping him all this time. I could do nothing to stop the first six murders — but if I can prevent number seven, I will."

"OK," Evra sighed. "Have it your own way."

"You won't interfere?"

"No," he promised.

"Even if I run into trouble and look like I need help?"

He hesitated before nodding. "All right. Not even then."

"You're a good friend, Evra," I said, clasping his hands.

"Think so?" He smiled bitterly. "Wait until you run foul of Mr Crepsley and end up trapped, screaming for help, only for me to ignore you. We'll see what sort of a friend you think I am then!"

# CHAPTER FOURTEEN

ON THE night of the twenty-second of December, Mr Crepsley made his move.

Evra spotted him. I was taking a short break, resting my eyes — even a half-vampire's eyes get sore after hours of concentration — when Evra gave a sudden alarmed jump and grabbed my ankle.

"He's moving!"

I sprang forward, just in time to see the vampire leaping on to the roof of the abattoir. He wrestled open a window and quickly slipped inside.

"This is it!" I moaned, leaping to my feet and setting off.

"Wait a sec," Evra said. "I'm coming with you."

"No!" I snapped. "We discussed this. You promised—"

"I won't come all the way in," Evra said. "But I'm not going to sit over here, worrying myself mad. I'll wait for you inside the abattoir."

There was no time to argue. Nodding curtly, I ran. Evra hurried after me as fast as he could.

I paused at the open window and listened carefully for sounds of the vampire. There were none. Evra pulled up beside me, gasping from the exertion of the run. I climbed in and Evra followed.

We found ourselves in a long room filled with pipes. The floor was covered in dust, in which Mr Crepsley's footprints were clearly visible. We traced the prints to a door, which opened on to a tiled corridor. The dust that Mr Crepsley's feet had picked up crossing the room now marked his path across the tiles.

We followed the dusty trail along the corridor and down a flight of stairs. We were in a quiet part of the abattoir – the workers were grouped near the other end – but we moved cautiously nevertheless: it wouldn't do to be caught at this delicate stage of the game.

As the dust grew fainter by the step, I worried about losing the vampire. I didn't want to have to cast blindly about the abattoir for him, so I quickened my pace. Evra matched me.

As we turned a corner, I glimpsed a familiar red cloak and promptly stopped. I stepped back out of sight, dragging Evra with me.

I mouthed the words, "Say nothing," then cautiously peered around the corner, to see what Mr Crepsley was up to.

The vampire was tucked behind cardboard boxes which were stacked against one of the walls. I saw nobody else, but I could hear footsteps approaching.

The fat man appeared through a door. He was whistling and looking through some papers attached to a clipboard which he was carrying. He stopped at a large automated door and pressed a button in the wall. With a sharp, grinding noise, it opened.

The fat man hung the clipboard on a hook on the wall, then entered. I heard him press a button on the other side. The door stopped, creaked and came down at the same slow pace with which it had gone up.

Mr Crepsley darted forward as the door was closing and slid underneath.

"Go back up to the room with the pipes and hide," I told Evra. He began to complain. "Just do it!" I snapped. "He'd spot you here on his way back if you stayed. Go up and wait. I'll track you down if I succeed in stopping him. If not..." I found his hands and squeezed hard. "It's been nice knowing you, Evra Von."

"Be careful, Darren," Evra said, and I could see the fear in his eyes. Not fear for himself. Fear for *me*. "Good luck."

"I don't need luck," I said bravely and pulled out my knife. "I've got this." Giving his hands another squeeze, I fled down the corridor and threw myself under the closing door, which soon shut behind me, locking me in with the fat man and the vampire.

The room was full of animal carcasses, which hung on steel hooks from the ceiling. It was refrigerated, to keep the animals fresh.

The stench of blood was ghastly. I knew the bodies were only those of animals, but I kept imagining they were humans.

The lights overhead were incredibly bright, so I had to move very carefully: a stray shadow could mean the end of me. The floor was slippery — water? blood? — so I had to watch where I put my feet.

There was a strange rosy glow around the carcasses, a result of the bright light and blood. You wouldn't want to be a vegetarian in a place like this!

After a few seconds of seeing nothing but dead animals, I spotted Mr Crepsley and the fat man. I fell in behind the pair and kept pace with them.

The fat man stopped and checked one of the carcasses. He

must have been feeling cold, because he blew into his hands to warm them up, even though he was wearing gloves. He gave the dead animal a slap when he finished examining it — the hook creaked creepily as the carcass swung to and fro — and began to whistle the same tune he'd been whistling outside.

He started walking again.

I was closing the gap between myself and Mr Crepsley — I didn't want to get left too far behind — when all of a sudden the fat man stooped to examine something on the ground. I stopped and began to slip back, afraid he'd spot my feet, then noticed Mr Crepsley creeping up on the crouching human.

I cursed beneath my breath and raced forward. If Mr Crepsley had been paying attention, he would have heard me, but he was concentrating on the man ahead.

I stopped a few metres behind the vampire and drew out my rusty knife. That would have been the perfect time to attack — the vampire was standing still, focused on the human, unaware of my presence, an ideal target — but I couldn't. Mr Crepsley had to make the first move. I'd refuse to believe the worst about him until he actually attacked. As Evra had said, if I killed him, there could be no bringing him back to life. This was no time to make a mistake.

The seconds seemed like hours as the fat man crouched, studying whatever it was that had grabbed his attention. Finally he shrugged and got back on his feet. I heard Mr Crepsley hiss and saw his body tense. I raised my knife.

The fat man must have heard something, because he looked up — the wrong way; he should have been looking backwards — an instant before Mr Crepsley leapt.

I'd been anticipating the move, but even so, I was wrong-footed. If I'd lunged at the same time as the vampire, I would have been able to lash out with the knife and hit where I was aiming: his throat. As it was, I hesitated a split second, which meant I was off target.

I yelled as I bounded after him, screaming loudly, partly to shock him out of his attack, partly because I was so horrified by what I was doing.

The scream caused Mr Crepsley to whip around. His eyes widened incredulously. Since he wasn't looking ahead any longer, he crashed awkwardly into the fat man and the two went sprawling to the ground.

I fell on Mr Crepsley and struck with the knife. The blade cut into the top of the vampire's left arm and bit deeply into his flesh. He roared with pain and tried shoving me off. I pushed him down – he was in a difficult position, his extra weight and strength no use to him – and drew back my arm, meaning to bring the knife down with all my force in a long, lethal strike.

I never made the killer cut. Because, as my arm flew back, it connected with somebody. Somebody floating downwards. Somebody who'd jumped from above. Somebody who screeched as my arm struck him, and rolled away from me as fast as he could.

Forgetting the vampire for a moment, I looked over my shoulder at the rolling figure. I could tell it was a man, but that was all I could tell until he stopped moving and got to his feet.

When he stood and looked at me, I found myself wishing he'd kept on rolling right out of the room.

He was a fearsome sight. A tall man. Broad and bloated. Dressed in white from head to ankle, an immaculate white suit, spoiled only by smudges of dirt and blood he'd picked up while rolling.

In total contrast to his white suit was his skin, hair, eyes, lips and nails. The skin was a blotchy purple colour. The rest were a dark, vibrant red, as though they'd been soaked in blood.

I didn't know who or what this creature was, but I could tell immediately that he was an agent of evil. It was written all over him, the way he stood, the way he sneered, the way madness danced in his unnatural red eyes, the way his ruby-red lips pulled back over his sharp, snarling teeth.

I heard Mr Crepsley curse and clamber to his feet. Before he got up, the white-suited man bellowed and ran towards me at a speed no human could have managed. He lowered his head and butted me, almost rupturing the walls of my stomach, driving the wind out of me.

I flew backwards, into Mr Crepsley, unwillingly driving him back to the floor.

The creature in white shrieked, hesitated a moment, as though contemplating an attack, then grabbed hold of a carcass and dragged himself up. He leapt up high and grabbed hold of a windowsill — for the first time, I realized windows ran around the entire top of the room — smashed the glass and slithered out.

Mr Crepsley cursed again and shoved me out of the way. He mounted a carcass and jumped up to the windowsill after the purple-skinned man, wincing from the pain in his injured left arm. He hung there a moment, listening intently. Then his head dropped and his shoulders sagged.

The fat human — who'd been blubbering like a baby — got to his knees and began crawling away. Mr Crepsley noticed him and, after one last desperate look through the window, dropped to the ground and hurried over to the man, who was trying to rise.

I watched helplessly as Mr Crepsley pulled the human up and glared into his face: if he was set on killing the man, there was nothing I could do to stop him. My ribs felt as though they'd been battered by a ram. Breathing was painful. Moving was out of the question.

But Mr Crepsley didn't have murder on his mind. All he did was breathe gas into the fat man's face, who stiffened, then slumped to the floor, unconscious.

Then Mr Crepsley whirled and advanced on me, rage in his eyes, the like of which I'd never seen before. I began to worry about my own life. He picked me up and shook me like a doll. "You idiot!" he roared. "You interfering, mindless fool! Do you realize what you have done? Do you?"

"I was ... trying to ... stop..." I wheezed. "I thought..."

Mr Crepsley pressed his face against mine and growled: "He has escaped! Because of your damned meddling, an insane killer has waltzed off scot-free! This was my chance to stop him and you ... you..."

He couldn't say any more: rage had seized his tongue. Dumping me to the ground, he spun away and sank to his haunches, cursing and groaning — at times he seemed to be almost crying — with undisguised disgust.

I looked from the vampire to the sleeping human to the broken window, and realized (it hardly took a genius to figure it out) that I'd made a dreadful — perhaps fatal — mistake.

# CHAPTER FIFTEEN

THERE WAS a long, edgy period of silence, minutes passing slowly. I felt around my ribs — none was broken. I stood and gritted my teeth as my insides flared with pain. I'd be tender for days to come.

Making my way over to Mr Crepsley, I cleared my throat. "Who *was* that?" I asked.

He glared at me and shook his head. "Idiot!" he growled. "What were you doing here?"

"Trying to stop you killing him," I said, pointing to the fat man. Mr Crepsley stared at me. "I heard about those six dead people on the news," I explained. "I thought you were the killer. I trailed—"

"You thought *I* was a murderer?" Mr Crepsley roared. I nodded glumly. "You are even dumber than I thought! Do you have so little faith in me that you—"

"What else was I to think?" I cried. "You never tell me anything. You disappeared into the city each night, not saying a thing about where you were going or what you were doing. What was I supposed to think when I heard six people had been found drained of their blood?"

Mr Crepsley looked startled, then thoughtful. Finally he nodded wearily. "You are right," he sighed. "One must show trust in order to be trusted. I wished to spare you the gory details. I should not have. This is my fault."

"That's OK," I said, taken aback by his gentle manner. "I guess I shouldn't have come after you like I did."

Mr Crepsley glanced at the knife. "You meant to kill me?" he asked.

"Yes," I said, embarrassed.

To my surprise, he chuckled dryly. "You are a reckless young man, Master Shan. But I knew that when I took you on as my assistant." He stood and examined the cut to his arm. "I suppose I should be grateful that I did not come out of this even worse."

"Will you be OK?" I asked.

"I will live," he said, rubbing spit into the cut, to heal it.

I looked up at the broken window. "Who *was* that?" I asked again.

"The question is not 'who'," Mr Crepsley said. "The question is 'what'. He is a *vampaneze*. His name is Murlough."

"What's a vampaneze?"

"It is a long story. We do not have time. Later, I will—"

"No," I said firmly. "I almost killed you tonight because I didn't know what was going on. Tell me about it *now*, so there can be no further mix-ups."

Mr Crepsley hesitated, then nodded. "Very well," he said. "I suppose here is as good a place as any. I do not think we will be disturbed. But we dare not delay. I must give this unwelcome turn of events much thought and begin planning anew. I will be brief. Try not to ask unnecessary questions."

"I'll try," I promised.

"The vampaneze are..." he searched for words. "In olden

nights, humans were looked down upon by many vampires, who fed on them as people feed on animals. It was not unusual for vampires to drink dry a couple of people a week. Over time, we decided this was not acceptable, so laws were established which forbade needless killing.

"Most vampires were content to obey the laws – it is easier for us to pass unnoticed amongst humans if we do not kill them – but some felt our cause had been betrayed. Certain vampires believed humans were put on this planet for us to feed upon."

"That's crazy!" I shouted. "Vampires start off as humans. What sort of—"

"Please," Mr Crepsley interrupted. "I am only trying to explain how these vampires thought. I am not condoning their actions.

"Seven hundred years ago, events came to a head. Seventy vampires broke away from the rest and declared themselves a separate race. They called themselves the vampaneze and established their own rules and governing bodies.

"Basically, the vampaneze believe it is wrong to feed from a human without killing. They believe there is nobility in draining a person and absorbing their spirit – as you absorbed part of Sam Grest's when you drank from him – and that there is shame in taking small amounts, feeding like a leech."

"So they always kill those they drink from?" I asked. Mr Crepsley nodded. "That's terrible!"

"I agree," the vampire said. "So did most of the vampires when the vampaneze broke away. There was a huge war. Many vampaneze were killed. Many vampires were too, but we were winning. We would have hunted them out of existence, except..." He smiled bitterly. "The humans we were trying to protect got in the way."

"What do you mean?" I asked.

"Many humans knew about vampires. But, as long as we did not kill them, they let us be — they were afraid of us. But when the vampaneze started slaughtering people, the humans panicked and fought back. Unfortunately they could not tell the difference between vampires and vampaneze, so both were tracked down and killed.

"We could have handled the vampaneze," Mr Crepsley said, "but not the humans. They were on the verge of wiping us out. In the end, our Princes met with the vampaneze and a truce was agreed. We would leave them alone if they stopped murdering so freely. They would only kill when they needed to feed, and would do all they could to keep their murders secret from humanity.

"The truce worked. When the humans realized they were safe, they stopped hunting us. The vampaneze travelled far away to avoid us — part of the agreement — and we have had virtually nothing to do with them for the last several centuries, apart from occasional clashes and challenges."

"*Challenges?*" I asked.

"Vampires and vampaneze live roughly," Mr Crepsley said. "We are forever testing ourselves in fights and competitions. Humans and animals are interesting opponents, but if a vampire really wants to test himself, he fights a vampaneze. It is common for vampires and vampaneze to seek each other out and fight to the death."

"That's stupid," I said.

Mr Crepsley shrugged. "It is our way. Time has changed the vampaneze," he went on. "You noticed the red hair and nails and eyes?"

"And lips," I added. "And he had purple skin."

"These changes have come about because they drink more

blood than vampires. Most vampaneze are not as colourful as Murlough — he has been drinking dangerously large amounts of blood — but they all have similar markings. Except for young vampaneze — it takes a couple of decades for the colours to set in."

I thought over what I'd been told. "So the vampaneze are evil? They're why vampires have such a bad reputation?"

Mr Crepsley rubbed his scar thoughtfully. "To say they are *evil* is not entirely true. To humans, they are, but to vampires they are more misdirected cousins than out-and-out ghouls."

"*What?*" I couldn't believe he was defending them.

"It depends on how one looks at it," he said. "You have learned to take no notice of drinking from humans, yes?"

"Yes," I said, "but—"

"Do you remember how against it you were in the beginning?"

"Yes," I said again, "but—"

"To many humans, *you* are evil," he said. "A young half-vampire who drinks human blood ... how long do you think it would be before somebody tried to kill you if your true identity was known?"

I chewed my lower lip and considered his words.

"Do not get me wrong," Mr Crepsley said. "I do not approve of the vampaneze and their ways. But nor do I think they are evil."

"You're saying it's OK to kill humans?" I asked warily.

"No," he disagreed. "I am saying I can see their point. Vampaneze kill because of their beliefs, not because they enjoy it. A human soldier who kills in war is not evil, is he?"

"This isn't the same thing," I said.

"But it falls along similarly murky lines. To humans, vampaneze are evil, plain and simple. But for vampires — and you belong to the vampire clan now – it is not so easy to judge. They are kin.

"Also," he added, "the vampaneze have their noble points. They are loyal and brave. And they never break their word – when a vampaneze makes a promise, he sticks by it. If a vampaneze lies, and his kinsmen find out, they will execute him, no questions asked. They have their faults, and I have no personal liking for them, but *evil*?" He sighed. "That is hard to say."

I frowned. "But you were going to kill this one," I reminded him.

Mr Crepsley nodded. "Murlough is not ordinary. Madness has invaded his mind. He has lost control and kills indiscriminately, feeding his lunatic lust. Were he a vampire, he would have been judged by the Generals and executed. The vampaneze, however, look more kindly upon their less fortunate members. They are loath to kill one of their own.

"If a vampaneze loses his mind, he is ejected from the ranks and set loose. If he keeps clear of his kind, they make no move to hinder or harm him. He is—"

A groan made us jump. Looking behind, we saw the fat man stirring.

"Come," Mr Crepsley said. "We will continue our discussion on the way to the roof."

We let ourselves out of the refrigerated room and started back.

"Murlough has been roaming the world for several years," Mr Crepsley said. "Normally, mad vampaneze do not last that long. They make silly mistakes and are soon caught and killed by humans. But Murlough is more cunning than most. He still has sense enough to kill quietly, and to hide the bodies. You know the myth about vampires not being able to enter a house unless they are invited inside?"

"Sure," I said. "I never believed it."

"Nor should you. But, like most myths, it has its roots in fact. The vampaneze almost never kill humans at home. They catch their prey outside, kill and feed, then hide the bodies, or disguise the wounds to make their death look accidental. Mad vampaneze normally forget these fundamental rules, but Murlough has remembered. That is how I knew he would not attack the man at home."

"How did you know he was going to attack him at all?" I asked.

"The vampaneze are traditionalists," Mr Crepsley explained. "They select their victims in advance. They sneak into their houses while the humans are sleeping and mark them – three small scratches on the left cheek. Did you notice such marks on the fat man?"

I shook my head. "I wasn't looking."

"They are there," Mr Crepsley assured me. "They are negligible – he probably thought he scratched himself while sleeping – but unmistakable once one knows what to look for: always in the same spot and always the same length.

"That is how I latched on to this man. Until that night I had been searching blindly, scouring the city, hoping to stumble across Murlough's trail. I spotted the fat man by chance and followed him. I knew the attack would come either here or on his way home from work, so it was just a matter of sitting back and waiting for Murlough to make his move." The vampire's face darkened. "Then *you* arrived on the scene." He was unable to keep the bitterness out of his voice.

"Will you be able to find Murlough again?" I asked.

He shook his head. "Discovering the marked human was

a stroke of incredible good fortune. It will not happen twice. Besides, though Murlough is mad, he is no fool. He will abandon any humans he has already marked and flee this city." Mr Crepsley sighed unhappily. "I suppose I will have to settle for that."

"*Settle* for it?" I asked. "Aren't you going to follow him?" Mr Crepsley shook his head. I stopped on the landing — we were almost at the door of the room with the pipes — and stared at him, aghast. "Why not?" I barked. "He's crazy! He's killing people! You've got to——"

"It is not my business," the vampire said gently. "It is not my place to worry about creatures such as Murlough."

"Then why get involved?" I cried, thinking of all the people the mad vampaneze was going to kill.

"The hands of the Vampire Generals are tied in matters such as these," Mr Crepsley said. "They dare not take steps to eliminate mad vampaneze, for fear of sparking an all-out war. As I said, vampaneze are loyal. They would seek revenge for the murder of one of their own. We can kill vampaneze in a fair fight, but if a General killed a mad vampaneze, his allies would feel compelled to strike back.

"I got involved because this is the city where I was born. I lived here as a human. Though everyone I knew then has long since died, I feel attached — this city, more than any place, is where I consider home.

"Gavner Purl knew this. When he realized Murlough was here, he set about tracking me down. He guessed — correctly — that I would not be able to sit back and let the mad vampaneze wreak havoc. It was a sly move on his part, but I do not blame him — in his position, I would have done the same."

"I don't get it," I said. "I thought the Vampire Generals wanted to avert a war."

"They do."

"But if you'd killed Murlough, wouldn't—"

"No," he interrupted. "I am not a General. I am a mere vampire, with no connection to any others. The vampaneze would have come after me if they learned I had killed him, but the Generals would not have been implicated. It would have been personal. It would not have led to war."

"I see. So, now that your city is safe, you don't care about him any more?"

"Yes," Mr Crepsley said simply.

I couldn't agree with the vampire's position – I'd have hunted Murlough down to the ends of the Earth – but I could understand it. He'd been protecting "his" people. Now that the threat against them had been removed, he no longer considered the vampaneze his problem. It was a typical piece of vampire logic.

"What happens now?" I asked. "We go back to the Cirque Du Freak and forget about this?"

"Yes," he said. "Murlough will avoid this city in future. He will slope away into the night and that will be that. We can return to our lives and get on with them."

"Until next time," I said.

"I have only one home," the vampire responded. "In all likelihood, there will be no next time. Come," he said. "If you have further questions, I will answer them later."

"OK." I paused. "What we said earlier – about no more holding important stuff back – is that still on? Will you trust me now and tell me things?"

The vampire smiled. "We will trust each other," he said.

I returned his smile and followed him, into the room with the pipes.

"How come I didn't spot Murlough's footsteps earlier?" I

asked, retracing the marks we'd made on our way into the building.

"He entered via a different route," Mr Crepsley said. "I did not want to get close to him until he made his move, in case he saw me."

I was on my way out of the window when I remembered Evra.

"Hold on!" I called Mr Crepsley back. "We've got to collect Evra."

"The snake-boy knew about this too?" Mr Crepsley laughed. "Hurry and get him. But do not expect me to tell the story again on his behalf. I will leave such details to you."

I cast around for my friend.

"Evra," I called quietly. When there was no response I shouted a little louder. "Evra!" Where was he hiding? I glanced down and found a lone pair of footprints in the dust, leading away under a mass of pipes.

"Evra!" I shouted again, starting after his trail. He'd probably seen me talking with the vampire and wasn't sure what was going on. "It's OK," I yelled. "Mr Crepsley isn't the killer. It's another—"

There was a sharp crunching noise as my foot came down on something and crushed it. Taking a step back, I bent and picked up the object for a closer examination. With a sinking feeling in my gut, I realized what it was — the broken remains of a mobile phone.

"Evra!" I screamed, dashing forward. I encountered signs of a scuffle further on — the dust in this area had been severely disturbed, as though somebody had been thrashing about in it. Thousands of dust motes were drifting in unsettled clouds through the air.

"What is it?" Mr Crepsley asked, approaching warily. I

showed him the crushed phone. "Evra's?" he guessed.

I nodded. "The vampaneze must have got him," I said, horrified.

Mr Crepsley sighed and hung his head. "Then Evra is dead," he said bluntly, and kept his gaze lowered as I started to cry.

# CHAPTER SIXTEEN

MR CREPSLEY booked us out of the hotel as soon as we got back, in case the staff noticed Evra's disappearance, or the vampaneze forced him to reveal our location.

"What if he escapes?" I asked. "How will he know where to find us?"

"I do not believe he will escape," Mr Crepsley said regretfully.

We checked into a new hotel not far from the old one. If the man behind the desk was surprised to find a solemn-looking man with a scar and a distraught young boy in a pirate costume booking in at such a strange hour, he kept his suspicions to himself.

I begged Mr Crepsley to tell me more about the vampaneze. He said they never drank from vampires – our blood was poisonous to other vampires and vampaneze. They lived slightly longer than vampires, though the difference was minimal. They ate very little food, preferring to keep going on blood. They only drank from animals as a last resort.

I listened closely. It was easier not to think about Evra if I had something else to focus on. But, when dawn came and Mr Crepsley headed for bed, I was left alone to dwell on what had happened.

I watched the sun rise. I was tired but unable to sleep. How could I face the nightmares that were surely lying in wait? I fixed a large breakfast, but my appetite fled after one small mouthful and I ended up tossing it in the bin. I switched on the TV and flicked between channels, barely noticing what was on.

Every so often I'd think it must have been a dream. Evra couldn't be dead. I'd fallen asleep on the roof while watching Mr Crepsley and dreamt it all. Any minute now, Evra would shake me awake. I'd tell him about my dream and we'd both laugh. "You won't get rid of me that easily," he'd chuckle.

But it wasn't a dream. I *had* come face to face with the mad vampaneze. He *had* abducted Evra. He *had* either killed him or was preparing to. These were facts and had to be faced.

The trouble was, I didn't dare face them. I was afraid I might go mad if I did. So, rather than accept the truth and deal with it, I buried it deep, where it couldn't bother me – then went to see Debbie. Maybe she could cheer me up.

Debbie was playing in the Square when I arrived. It had snowed heavily during the night and she was building a snowman with some of the local kids. She was surprised but happy to see me so early. She introduced me to her friends, who regarded me curiously.

"Want to come for a walk?" I asked.

"Can it wait till I finish the snowman?" she replied.

"No," I said. "I'm restless. I need to walk. I can come back later if you want."

"That's all right. I'll come." She looked at me oddly. "Are you OK? Your face is white as a sheet, and your eyes ... have you been crying?"

"I was peeling onions earlier," I lied.

Debbie turned to her friends. "See you later," she said, and took my arm. "Anywhere special you want to go?"

"Not really," I said. "You lead. I'll tag along."

We didn't say much while we were walking, until Debbie tugged my arm and said, "I've got some good news. I asked Mum and Dad if you could come over on Christmas Eve to help put up the decorations and they said you could."

"Great," I said, forcing a smile.

"They've invited you for dinner too," she said. "They were going to ask you over for Christmas Day, but I know you've made plans to spend it in the hotel. Besides, I don't think your dad would want to come, would he?"

"No," I said softly.

"But Christmas Eve's OK, isn't it?" she asked. "Evra can come as well. We'll be eating early, about two or three in the afternoon, so there'll be plenty of time for decorating the trees. You can—"

"Evra won't be able to come," I said shortly.

"Why not?"

I found myself struggling to think up a suitable lie. Finally, I said, "He's got flu. He's in bed and can't move."

"He seemed fine yesterday," Debbie frowned. "I saw the two of you going out in the evening. He looked—"

"How did you see us?" I asked.

"Through the window," she said. "It's not the first time I've noticed you going out after dark. I never said anything about it before, because I thought you'd have told me what you were up to if you'd wanted me to know."

"It's not nice to spy on people," I snapped.

"I wasn't spying!" Debbie looked hurt by my accusation and tone. "I just happened to see you. And if that's going to be your attitude, you can forget Christmas Eve." She turned to leave.

"Wait," I said, catching her arm (careful not to grab too hard). "I'm sorry. I'm in a really bad mood. I don't feel so good. Maybe I've picked up something from Evra."

"You *do* look under the weather," she agreed, her face softening.

"As for where we go at night, it's just to meet our dad," I said. "We join him after work and go out for something to eat, or to see a movie. I'd have invited you along, but you know how things stand with my dad."

"You should introduce us," Debbie said. "I bet I'd be able to get him to like me, if I only had the chance."

We started walking again.

"So, how about Christmas Eve?" she asked.

I shook my head. Sitting down to dinner with Debbie and her parents was the last thing I wanted to think about. "I'll have to get back to you on that one," I said. "I'm not sure if we'll be here. We might be moving on."

"But Christmas Eve is tomorrow!" Debbie exclaimed. "Surely your dad's told you his plans by now."

"He's strange," I said. "He likes to leave things till the very last minute. I could arrive back after this walk and find him packed and ready to go."

"He can't leave if Evra's sick," she said.

"He can and will, if he wants," I told her.

Debbie frowned and stopped walking. There was a street grille a metre or so over, out of which warm air was blowing. She moved closer to it and stood on the bars. "You won't leave without telling me, will you?" she asked.

"Of course not," I said.

"I'd hate it if you disappeared into thin air without a word," she said, and I could see tears gathering in the corners of her eyes.

"I promise," I said. "When *I* know I'm leaving, *you'll* know too. Word of honour." I crossed my heart.

"Come here," she said, and pulled close and gave me a big hug.

"What was that for?" I asked.

"Does there have to be a reason?" she smiled, then pointed ahead. "Let's turn at the next corner. That'll lead us back to the Square."

I took Debbie's arm, meaning to walk her back, then remembered I'd changed hotels. If I returned to the Square, she'd expect me to enter the hotel. She might grow suspicious if she spotted me skulking away.

"I'll carry on walking," I said. "I'll ring tonight or in the morning to let you know whether I can come round tomorrow or not."

"If your Dad wants to leave, try twisting his arm to get him to stay," she suggested. "I'd really love to have you over."

"I'll try," I vowed, and watched through sad eyes as she strolled to the corner and turned out of sight.

It was then that I heard a soft chuckling noise beneath my feet. Glancing down through the bars of the grille, I saw nobody, and thought I must have been hearing things. But then a voice came up out of the shadows.

"I like your girlfriend, Darren Shan," it giggled, and I knew instantly who was down there. "A very tasty dish. Good enough to eat, wouldn't you say? Much tastier-looking than your other friend. Much tastier than Evra."

It was Murlough — the mad vampaneze!

# CHAPTER SEVENTEEN

I DROPPED to my knees and peered through the bars of the grille. It was dark down there, but after a few seconds I was able to make out the rough figure of the fat vampaneze.

"What's your girlfriend's name, hmmm?" Murlough asked. "Anne? Beatrice? Catherine? Diane? Elsa? Franny? Geraldine? Henrietta? Eileen? Josie—" He stopped and I could sense him frowning. "No. Wait. Eileen begins with an 'E', not an 'I'. Are there any women's names beginning with 'I'? I can't think of any off-hand. How about you, Darren Shan? Any ideas, hmmm? Any notions?" He pronounced my first name oddly, so that it rhymed with Jarwren.

"How did you find me?" I gasped.

"That was easy." He leaned forward, carefully avoiding the rays of sunlight, and tapped the side of his head. "Used my brains," he said. "Young Murlough's got plenty of brains, yes he does. I played a tune on your friend – Snakey Von. He told me where the hotel was. I set up camp outside. Watched carefully. Saw you passing with your girlfriend, so I followed."

"What do you mean, 'Played a tune'?" I asked.

The vampaneze laughed out loud. "With my knife," he explained. "My knife and a few sets of scales. Get it? *Scales.* Scales on Snakey, scales on a piano. Ha! Brains, I told you, brains! A stupid man couldn't make jokes so cunning, jokes so shrewd. Young Murlough has brains the size of—"

"Where's Evra?" I interrupted, pounding the bars of the grille to shut him up. I gave them a yank, to see if I could get down to him, but they were set firm in the path.

"Evra? Evra Von?" Murlough did a strange little half-dance in the darkness beneath the grille. "Evra's strapped up," he told me. "Hanging by his ankles. Blood rushing to his head. Squealing like a piggie. Begging to be let free."

"Where is he?" I asked desperately. "Is he alive?"

"Tell me," he said, ignoring my questions, "where are you and the vampire staying? You've moved hotels, haven't you? That's why I didn't see you coming out. What were you doing in the Square anyway? No!" he shouted as I opened my mouth to speak. "Don't tell me, don't tell me! Give the brains a chance to work. Young Murlough's got plenty of brains. Brains oozing out his ears, some would say."

He paused, his little eyes darting to and fro, then clicked his fingers and hooted. "The girl! Darren Shan's little friend! She lives in the Square, hmmm? You wanted to see her. Which house is hers? Don't tell me, don't tell me! I'll figure it out. I'll track her down. Juicy-looking girl. Plenty of blood, hmmm? Lovely salty blood. I can taste her already."

"Stay away from her!" I screamed. "If you go near her, I'll—"

"Shut up!" the vampaneze barked. "Don't threaten me! I won't take lip from a runtish half-vampire like you. Any more like that and I'm off, and that'll be the end of Snakey."

I brought myself under control. "Does that mean he's

still alive?" I asked shakily.

Murlough grinned and tapped his nose. "Maybe he is, maybe he isn't. No way for you to know for sure, is there?"

"Mr Crepsley said vampaneze have to keep their word," I said. "If you give me your word that he's alive, then I'll know."

Murlough nodded slowly. "He's alive."

"You give me your word?"

"I give you my word," he said. "Snakey's alive. Trussed up and strung up. Squealing like a piggie. I'm keeping him for Christmas. He'll be my Christmas dinner. Snakey instead of turkey. Do you think that's foul of me, hmmm?" He laughed. "Get it? *Foul*. Not one of my subtler jokes, but it'll do. Snakey laughed. Snakey does everything I tell him to. You would too, in his position. Dangling by his ankles. Squealing like a piggie."

Murlough had an irritating way of repeating himself.

"Look," I said, "let Evra go. Please, he's done you no harm."

"He interfered with my schedule!" the vampaneze shrieked. "I was ready to feed. It was going to be glorious. I would have drained the fat man, then skinned him alive and stuck his corpse up with the rest in the cold room. Made cannibals of some poor unsuspecting humans. It would have been great sport, hmmm?"

"Evra didn't get in your way," I said. "That was me and Mr Crepsley. Evra was outside."

"*In*side, *out*side – he wasn't on *my* side. But he soon will be." Murlough licked his blood-red lips. "On my side and in my tummy. I never had snake-boy before. I'm looking forward to it. Maybe I'll stuff him before feeding. Make it more Christmassy."

"I'll kill you!" I screamed, tugging at the grille again, losing my self-control. "I'll track you down and tear you apart, limb from limb!"

"Oh my!" Murlough laughed, pretending to be scared. "Oh

heavens! Please don't hurt me, nasty little half-vampire. Young Murlough's a good chap. Say you'll leave me be."

"Where's Evra?" I roared. "Bring him up here now, or I'll—"

"All right," Murlough snapped, "that's enough! I didn't come here to be shouted at, no I didn't. There's plenty of other places I can go if I want people shouting at me, hmmm? Now shut up and listen."

It took a lot of effort, but I finally managed to calm down.

"Good," Murlough grunted. "That's better. You're not as stupid as most vampires. A bit of brains in Darren Shan, hmmm? Not as smart as me, of course, but who is? Young Murlough's got more brains than...

"Enough." He dug his nails into the wall beneath the grille and climbed up a couple of metres. "Listen carefully." He sounded sane now. "I don't know how you found me — Snakey couldn't tell me, no matter how many scales I played — and I don't care. That's your secret. Keep it. We all need secrets, don't we, hmmm?

"And I don't care about the human," he went on. "He was just a meal. Plenty more where he came from. Plenty more blood in the fleshy human sea.

"I don't even care about *you*," he snorted. "Half-vampires don't interest me. You were only following your master. You don't worry me. I'm prepared to let you live. You and Snakey and the human.

"But the vampire — Larten Crepsley." The vampaneze's red eyes filled with hate. "*Him* I care about. He should have known better than to get in my way. Vampires and vampaneze don't mix!" he roared at the top of his voice. "Even the fools of the world know that! It's been agreed upon. We don't interfere with one another's ways. He broke the laws. He must be made to pay."

"He broke no law," I said defiantly. "You're mad. You were killing people all over the city. You had to be stopped."

"*Mad?*" I'd expected Murlough to react furiously to the insult, but he only chuckled. "Is that what he told you? *Mad?* Young Murlough isn't mad! I'm as sane a vampaneze as ever walked. Would I be here if I was mad? Would I have had sense enough to keep Snakey alive? Do you see me foaming at the mouth? Do you hear me gabbling like an idiot? Hmmm?"

I decided to humour him. "Maybe not," I said. "You seem pretty smart now that I think about it."

"Of course I'm smart! Young Murlough's got brains. Can't be mad if you've got brains, not unless you get rabies. See any rabid animals?"

"No," I said.

"There you are!" he declared triumphantly. "No crazy animals, so no crazy Murlough. You follow, hmmm?"

"I follow," I said quietly.

"Why did he interfere?" Murlough asked. He sounded confused and petulant. "I was doing nothing to him. I wouldn't have got in his way. What did he have to go and mess things up for?"

"This used to be his city," I explained. "He lived here when he was a human. He felt it was his duty to protect the people."

Murlough stared at me incredulously. "You mean he did it for *them?*" he screeched. "The *blood-carriers?*" He laughed crazily. "He must be a loony! I thought maybe he wanted them for himself. Or else I'd killed somebody close to him. I never for a second thought he did it because of ... of..."

Murlough started laughing. "That clinches it," he said. "I can't let a lunatic like that run around. No telling what he'll get up to next. Listen to me, Darren Shan. You look like a smart boy. Let's you and me do a deal. Sort this mess out, hmmm?"

"What sort of a deal?" I asked suspiciously.

"A swap," Murlough said. "I know where Snakey is. You know where the vampire is. One for the other. What do you say?"

"Give up Mr Crepsley for Evra?" I sneered. "What sort of a deal is that? Exchange one friend for another? You can't believe I'd—"

"Why not?" Murlough asked. "The snake-boy is innocent, hmmm? Your best friend, he told me. The vampire's the one who took you away from your family, from your home. Evra told me you hated him."

"That was a long time ago," I said.

"Even so," the vampaneze went on, "if you had to choose between the two, who would you pick? If their lives hung in the balance and you could only save one, who would it be?"

I didn't have to consider that very long. "Evra," I said evenly.

"There you are!" Murlough boomed.

"But Mr Crepsley's life *isn't* in danger," I said. "You want me to use him to get Evra off the hook." I shook my head sadly. "I won't do that. I won't betray him or lead him into a trap."

"You don't have to," Murlough said. "Just tell me where he is. The name of the hotel and his room number. I'll do the rest. I'll sneak in while he's sleeping, do the business, then take you to get Evra. I give you my word that I'll let both of you go. Think about it, hmmm? Weigh up the options. The vampire or Snakey. Your choice."

Again I shook my head. "No. There's nothing to think about. I'll swap places with Evra myself, if that—"

"I don't care about *you!*" Murlough screamed. "It's the vampire I want. What would I do with a stupid little half-vampire? Can't drink from you. Nothing to gain by killing you. It's Crepsley or no deal."

"Then it's no deal," I said, sobs rising in my throat as I considered what my words meant for Evra.

Murlough spat at me in disgust. His spit bounced back off the grille. "You're a fool," he snarled. "I thought you were smart, but you're not. So be it. I'll find the vampire myself. Your girlfriend, too. I'll kill them both. Then I'll kill you. Wait and see if I don't."

The vampaneze let go of the wall and dropped into the darkness. "Think of me, Darren Shan," he shouted as he slipped away down a tunnel. "Think of me when Christmas comes round, as you're biting into your turkey and ham. Do you know what *I'll* be biting into? Do you?" His laugh echoed eerily as he waltzed away down the tunnel.

"Yes," I said softly. I knew exactly what he'd be biting into.

Getting to my feet, I wiped the tears from my face, then set off to wake Mr Crepsley and tell him about my meeting with Murlough. After a couple of minutes, I climbed up a fire escape and travelled over the rooftops, just in case the vampaneze had stuck around in the hope of following me back.

# CHAPTER EIGHTEEN

MR CREPSLEY wasn't surprised that Murlough had been watching the hotel — he'd half-expected it — but *was* stunned that I'd gone back to the Square.

"What were you thinking of?" he snapped.

"You didn't warn me to stay away," I replied.

"I did not think I needed to," he groaned. "What could have possessed you to return?"

I decided it was time to tell him about Debbie. He listened wordlessly as I explained.

"A girlfriend," he said at the end, shaking his head wonderingly. "Why did you think I would disapprove? There is no reason you should not befriend a girl. Even full-vampires sometimes fall in love with humans. It is complicated, and not to be recommended, but there is nothing wrong with it."

"You're not angry?" I asked.

"Why should I be? Matters of your heart are no concern of mine. You acted properly: you made no promises you could not keep, and you remained aware of the fact that it could only be temporary. All that worries me about your friendship with this girl is how it ties in with the vampaneze."

"You think Murlough will go after her?"

"I doubt it," he said. "I think he will stay clear of the Square. Now that we know he has been there, he will expect us to check on the area in future. However, you should be careful. Do not go to see her when it is dark. Enter by the back door. Keep away from the windows."

"It's OK for me to go on meeting her?" I asked.

"Yes," he smiled. "I know you consider me something of a killjoy, but I would never intentionally make you feel miserable."

I smiled back gratefully.

"And Evra?" I asked. "What will happen to him?"

Mr Crepsley's smile faded. "I am not sure." He thought about it for a couple of minutes. "You truly refused to swap my life for his?" He sounded as if he thought I might be making it up to impress him.

"Honestly," I said.

"But *why*?"

I shrugged. "We said we'd trust each other, remember?"

Mr Crepsley turned aside and coughed into his fist. When he faced me again, he looked ashamed of himself. "I have gravely underestimated you, Darren," he said. "I will not do so again. I made a wiser choice than I realized when I chose you to serve as my assistant. I feel honoured to have you by my side."

The compliment made me feel awkward – I wasn't used to the vampire saying nice things – so I grimaced and tried to make little of it.

"What about Evra?" I asked again.

"We shall do what we can to rescue him," Mr Crepsley said. "It is unfortunate that you refused to swap me for him: had we known Murlough would make the offer, we could have laid a trap. Now that you have shown loyalty towards me, he will not offer again. Our best chance to beat him has slipped away.

"But there is hope yet," he said. "Today is the twenty-third. We know that Evra will not be killed before the twenty-fifth."

"Unless Murlough changes his mind," I said.

"Unlikely. The vampaneze are not renowned for being indecisive. If he said he would not kill Evra until Christmas Day, that is when he will kill him. We have all tonight and tomorrow night to search for his lair."

"But he could be anywhere in the city!" I cried.

"I disagree," Mr Crepsley said. "He is not *in* the city — he is *under* it. Holed up in the tunnels. The drainpipes. The sewers. Hiding from the sun, free to move about as he wishes."

"You can't know that for sure," I said. "He might have only been down there today in order to follow me."

"If he was," Mr Crepsley said, "we are sunk. But if he *has* made his base down there, we stand a chance. Space is not so plentiful beneath the ground. Noises are easier to detect. It will not be easy, but there is hope. Last night, we did not even have that.

"If all else fails," he added, "and we end up empty-handed..." His face hardened. "I will call to our murderous cousin and offer him the deal which you yourself put to him earlier."

"You mean...?"

"Yes," he said darkly. "If we do not find Evra in time, I will trade *my* life for his."

There was more space beneath the ground than Mr Crepsley had predicted. It was an endless twisting maze down there. The pipes seemed to go every which way, as though thrown down at random. Some were big enough to stand in, others barely large enough to crawl through. Many were in use, half-full of streams of water and waste. Others were old and dried-up and cracked.

The stench was terrible. One thing was certain: we might happen to hear or glimpse Murlough or Evra, but we'd certainly never be able to sniff them out!

The place was awash with rats and spiders and insects. But I soon discovered that if you ignored them, they generally ignored you back.

"I do not understand why they need so many tunnels," Mr Crepsley said grimly, after several hours of fruitless searching. We seemed to have walked halfway across the city, but when he stuck his head above ground to check our position, he found we'd come less than three-quarters of a kilometre.

"I guess different tunnels were made at different times," I said. My dad used to work for a building firm and had explained a bit about underground systems to me. "They wear out in places, eventually, and it's usually easier to dig new shafts than go back and patch up the old ones."

"What a waste," Mr Crepsley grumbled, disdainfully. "You could fit a small town into the space these damned pipes are taking up." He looked around. "There seem to be more holes than concrete," he said. "I am surprised the city has not fallen in upon itself."

After a while, Mr Crepsley stopped and cursed.

"Do you want to stop?" I asked.

"No," he sighed. "We shall continue. It is better to search than sit back and wait. At least this way we are exerting some sort of control over our destiny."

We used torches in the tunnels. We needed some sort of light: even vampires can't see in total darkness. The beams increased the chances of Murlough's spotting us before we spotted him, but that was a risk we had to take.

"There's no way of hunting him down telepathically, is there?" I asked as we paused for a break. All this crawling and stooping was exhausting. "Couldn't you search for his thoughts?"

The vampire shook his head. "I have no connection with Murlough," he said. "Tuning into a person's mental signals requires radar-like emissions on both sides." He held up his two index fingers about half a metre apart. "Say this is me." He wiggled his right finger. "This is Mr Tall." He wiggled the left. "Many years ago, we learnt to recognize each other's mental waves. Now, if I want to find Mr Tall, I emit a radar-like series of waves." He bent his right finger up and down. "When these signals connect with Hibernius, part of his mind automatically signals back, even if his conscious mind remains unaware of it."

"You mean you could find him even if he didn't want to be found?"

Mr Crepsley nodded. "That is why most people refuse to share their wave identity. You should only reveal it to one you truly trust. Less than ten people on Earth can find me that way, or I them." He smiled thinly. "Needless to say, none of those ten is a vampaneze."

I wasn't sure I understood entirely about mental waves, but I'd gathered enough to know Mr Crepsley couldn't use it to find Evra.

One more hope struck from the list.

But the conversation had set me thinking. I was sure there must be some way of bettering the odds. Mr Crepsley's plan — to roam the tunnels and pray we fell upon the vampaneze — was weak. Was there nothing else we could do? No way to prepare a trap and lure Murlough into it?

I focused my immediate thoughts on the search — if we stumbled upon the mad vampaneze, I didn't want to be caught with my head in the clouds – but devoted the rest to serious thinking.

Something the vampaneze had said was niggling away at the back of my brain, but I couldn't put my finger on it. I went back over everything he'd said. We'd talked about Evra and Mr Crepsley and Debbie and doing a deal and...

*Debbie.*

He'd teased me about her, said he was going to kill and drink from her. At the time I'd dismissed it as an idle threat, but the more I thought about it, the more I began to wonder how much he really was interested in her.

He would be hungry, down here in the depths. He was used to feeding regularly. We'd ruined his schedule. He'd said he was looking forward to drinking Evra's blood, but *was* he? Vampires couldn't drink from snakes and I was willing to bet vampaneze couldn't either. Maybe Evra's blood would prove undrinkable. Perhaps Murlough would only be able to kill the snake-boy on Christmas Day, not drink from him as planned. He'd commented a couple of times on how tasty Debbie looked. Was that a clue that Evra *didn't* look tasty?

As the time ticked by, thoughts turned over in my head. I said nothing when Mr Crepsley told me we should return to the surface (he had a natural in-built clock), in case Murlough was shadowing us and listening to our every word. I kept quiet as we climbed out of the tunnel and trudged through the streets, then took to the roofs again. I held my tongue as we sneaked through our hotel window and sank into chairs, tired, miserable and gloomy.

But then, hesitantly, I coughed to attract the vampire's attention. "I think I have a plan," I said, and slowly spelt it out for him.

# CHAPTER NINETEEN

JESSE ANSWERED the phone when I rang Debbie's house. I asked if I could speak to her. "You could if she was up," he laughed. "Do you know what time it is?"

I checked my watch: a few minutes before seven a.m. "Oh," I said, crestfallen. "Sorry. I didn't realize. Did I wake you?"

"No," he said. "I have to pop into the office, so it's business as usual for me. You just caught me, in fact – I was on my way out the door when the phone rang."

"You're working on Christmas Eve?"

"No rest for the wicked," he laughed. "But I'll only be there a couple of hours. Tying up some loose ends before the Christmas break. I'll be back in plenty of time for dinner. Speaking of which, are we to expect you or not?"

"Yes please," I said. "That's why I was ringing, to say I could come."

"Great!" He sounded genuinely pleased. "How about Evra?"

"Can't make it," I said. "He's still not well."

"Too bad. Listen, do you want me to wake Debbie? I can—"

"That's OK," I said quickly. "Just let her know I'll be there. Two o'clock?"

"Two's fine," Jesse said. "See you later, Darren."

"Bye, Jesse."

I hung up and went straight to bed. My head was still buzzing from all the talking me and Mr Crepsley had been doing, but I forced my eyes shut and concentrated on sweet thoughts. Moments later, my tired body drifted off to sleep and I slept soundly until one in the afternoon, when the alarm clock went off.

My ribs were aching as I got up and my belly was purple and blue with bruises, where Murlough had head-butted me. It wasn't too bad after a few minutes of walking about, but I was careful not to make any sudden movements, and bent down as little as possible.

I had a good shower, and sprayed deodorant all over myself when I was dry – the smell of the sewers was hard to get rid of. I dressed, and picked up a bottle of wine Mr Crepsley had bought for me to take to Debbie's.

I knocked on Debbie's back door as Mr Crepsley had advised. Donna opened it. "Darren!" she said, kissing me on both cheeks. "Merry Christmas!"

"Merry Christmas," I replied in return.

"Why didn't you use the front door?" she asked.

"I didn't want to dirty your carpets," I said, scraping my shoes on the mat inside the door. "My shoes are wet from the dirty slush."

"Silly," she smiled. "As if anyone cares about carpets at Christmas. Debbie!" she called upstairs. "There's a handsome pirate here to see you."

"Hi," Debbie said, coming down the stairs. She kissed me on both cheeks as well. "Dad told me you rang. What's in the bag?"

I produced the bottle of wine. "For dinner," I said. "My dad gave it to me to bring over."

"Oh, Darren, that's kind," said Donna. She took the wine and called to Jesse, "Look what Darren brought."

"Ah! Vino!" Jesse's eyes lit up. "Better than the wine we'd got in. We invited the right man over. We should have him round more often. Where's the corkscrew?"

"Wait a while," Donna laughed. "Dinner isn't ready yet. I'll stick it in the fridge. You lot head for the living room. I'll yell when it's time."

We pulled some crackers while we were waiting, and Debbie asked me if my dad had decided about moving on yet. I said he had, and that we were leaving tonight.

"*Tonight?*" She looked dismayed. "Nobody travels anywhere except home on Christmas Eve. I've a good mind to go over to that hotel, drag him out and—"

"That's where we're going," I interrupted. "Home. Mum and Dad are getting together again, just for Christmas Day, to give Evra and me a treat. It's supposed to be a surprise, but I heard him on the phone this morning. That's why I rang so early – I was excited."

"Oh." I could tell Debbie was upset by the news, but she put on a brave face. "That's wonderful. I bet it's the best present you could have hoped for. Maybe they'll patch things up and get back together for good."

"Maybe," I said.

"So this is your last afternoon together," Jesse remarked. "Fate has driven the young romantics apart."

"*Da-a-a-ad!*" Debbie moaned, punching him. "Don't say things like that! It's embarrassing!"

"That's what fathers are for," Jesse grinned. "It's our job to embarrass our daughters in front of boyfriends."

Debbie scowled at him, but I could see she was enjoying the attention.

The meal was magnificent. Donna had put all her years of expertise to great use. The turkey and ham practically melted in my mouth. The roast potatoes were crisp and the veg was sweet as candyfloss. Everything looked wonderful and tasted even better.

Jesse told a few jokes which had us all in stitches, and Donna did her party trick: balancing a roll on her nose. Debbie took a mouthful of water and gargled her way through *Silent Night*. Then it was my turn to do a bit of entertaining.

"This meal is so good," I sighed, "I could even eat the cutlery." While everybody laughed, I picked up a spoon, bit off the head, chewed it into tiny pieces, and swallowed.

Three pairs of eyes practically popped out of their sockets.

"How did you do that?" Debbie squealed.

"You pick up more than dust when you're on the road," I said, winking at her.

"It was a fake spoon!" Jesse roared. "He's having us on."

"Hand me yours," I told him. He hesitated, tested his spoon to make sure it was real, then passed it over. It didn't take long to gulp it down, my tough vampire teeth making short work of it.

"That's incredible!" Jesse gasped, clapping wildly. "Let's try him with a ladle."

"Hold it!" Donna yelled as Jesse reached across the table. "These are part of a set and hard to replace. You'll be letting him loose on my grandmother's good china next."

"Why not?" Jesse said. "I never did like those old plates."

"Watch it," Donna warned, tweaking his nose, "or I'll make *you* eat the plates."

Debbie was smiling, and leant over to squeeze my hand.

"I feel thirsty after those spoons," I joked, getting to my feet. "I think it's time for my wine now."

"Hear, hear!" Jesse cheered.

"I can get it," Donna said, rising.

"Not at all," I said, gently pushing her back down. "You've been serving all afternoon. It's time someone waited on you for a change."

"Hear that?" Donna beamed at the other two. "I think I'll exchange Debbie for Darren. He'd be much more useful to have around."

"That's it!" Debbie snorted. "No presents for *you* tomorrow!"

I was smiling to myself as I fetched the wine from the fridge and peeled back the tin-foil from the top. The corkscrew was in the sink. I rinsed it, then opened the bottle. I sniffed — I didn't know much about wine, but it certainly smelt nice — and found four clean glasses. I rooted through my pockets for a couple of seconds, then fiddled with three of the glasses. Next I poured the wine and returned to the table.

"Hurrah!" Jesse shouted when he saw me coming.

"What took you so long?" Debbie asked. "We were about to send a search party to look for you."

"Took me a while to get the cork out," I said. "I'm not used to it."

"You should have just bitten the top off," Jesse joked.

"I didn't think of that," I said seriously. "I'll do it next time. Thanks for the advice."

Jesse stared at me uncertainly. "Nearly had me going!" he laughed suddenly, shaking a finger, "Nearly had me going!"

His brief bit of repetition reminded me momentarily of Murlough, but I swiftly put all thoughts of the vampaneze from my mind and raised my glass.

"A toast," I declared. "To the Hemlocks. Their name might be poison, but their hospitality is first class. Cheers!" I'd rehearsed the toast earlier, and it went down as well as I'd hoped. They groaned, then laughed and raised their glasses, clinking them against mine.

"Cheers," Debbie said.

"Cheers," Donna added.

"Bottoms up!" Jesse chuckled.

And we drank.

# CHAPTER TWENTY

*Late Christmas Eve. Down in the tunnels.*

WE'D BEEN searching for a couple of hours, but it felt longer. We were sweating and covered with dirt, our feet and trousers soaked through with filthy water. We were moving as fast as we could, making a lot of noise in the process. My ribs hurt me to begin with, but I was over the worst of it now and barely noticed the stabbing pain as I bent and stooped and twisted.

"Slow down!" Mr Crepsley hissed several times. "He will hear us if you keep this up. We must be more careful."

"To hell with being careful!" I yelled back. "This is our last chance to find him. We've got to cover as much ground as possible. I don't care how much noise we make."

"But if Murlough hears us—" Mr Crepsley began.

"—We'll chop off his head and stuff it with garlic!" I snarled, and moved ahead even faster, making still more noise.

Soon we reached a particularly large tunnel. The water level was higher in most of the tunnels than it had been last night, because of the melting snow on the ground, but this one was dry. Perhaps it was an emergency pipe, in case the others overflowed.

"We will rest here," Mr Crepsley said, collapsing. The search was harder for him than for me, since he was taller and had to bend more.

"We don't have time for a rest," I snapped. "Do you think Murlough is resting?"

"Darren, you must calm down," Mr Crepsley said. "I understand your agitation, but we cannot help Evra by panicking. You are tired, as am I. A few minutes will make no difference, one way or the other."

"You don't care, do you?" I sulked. "Evra's down here somewhere, being tormented or cooked, and all you're worried about are your tired old legs."

"They *are* old," Mr Crepsley growled, "and they *are* tired, and so, I am sure, are yours. Sit down and stop acting like a child. If we are destined to find Evra, we shall. If not..."

I snarled hatefully at the vampire and stepped in front of him. "Give me that torch," I said, trying to prise it from his hands. I'd dropped mine earlier and broken it. "I'll go on ahead by myself. You sit here and *rest*. I'll find Evra on my own."

"Stop it," Mr Crepsley said, pushing me away. "You are behaving intolerably. Calm down and——"

I gave a ferocious tug and the torch flew out of Mr Crepsley's hands. It also spun out of mine, and shattered to pieces against the tunnel wall. We were thrust into complete darkness.

"You idiot!" Mr Crepsley roared. "Now we will have to go back up and find a replacement. You have cost us time. I told you something like this would happen."

"Shut up!" I shouted, shoving the vampire in the chest. He fell down hard and I backed away blindly.

"Darren!" Mr Crepsley shouted. "What are you doing?"

"Going to find Evra," I said.

"You cannot! Not by yourself! Come back and help me up: I have twisted my ankle. We will return with stronger torches and work faster. You cannot search without a light."

"I can hear," I replied. "And I can feel. And I can shout. Evra!" I yelled, to prove my point. "Evra! Where are you? It's me!"

"Stop! Murlough will hear. Come back and keep quiet!"

I heard the vampire scrabbling to his feet. Taking a deep breath, I ran. I fled far into the tunnel, then slowed and found a small pipe leading out of the large one. I slipped into it and crawled. Mr Crepsley's shouts grew dimmer and dimmer. Then I came to another pipe, and scurried down it. Then another. And another. Within five minutes I'd lost the vampire.

I was alone. In the dark. Underground.

I shivered, then reminded myself why I was there and what was at stake. I scouted about for a larger tunnel, feeling my way with my fingers.

"Evra," I called softly. I cleared my throat and this time yelled. "Evra! It's me! Darren! Can you hear? I'm coming to find you. Yell if you can hear me. Evra. Evra? Evra!"

Shouting and calling, I advanced, hands outstretched, ears straining for any sound, eyes useless – a perfect target for all the demons of the dark.

I'm not sure how long I was down there. There was no way of telling time in the tunnels. I had no sense of direction either. I might have been going in circles. I just moved forward, calling Evra's name, scraping my hands on the walls, feeling my feet and lower legs turn numb from the damp and cold.

Sometimes a draught of air tickled my nostrils, a reminder

of the world above. I moved fast whenever I felt the air, afraid of losing my nerve if I stopped to breathe it in.

I was moving downwards, getting deeper into the system of pipes and tunnels. I wondered how many people had been down here over the years. Not many. In some of the older pipes, I might be the first human (*half*-human) to pass in decades. If I'd had time, I would have stopped to scrawl my initials on the walls.

"Evra! Can you hear me? Evra!" I repeated.

There'd been no response so far. I wasn't really expecting one. If I did chance upon Murlough's lair, it was a pretty sure thing he would have taped over Evra's mouth. The vampaneze wasn't the sort to overlook a minor detail like that.

"*Evra!*" I croaked, my voice beginning to crack from the strain. "Are you there? Can you—"

All of a sudden, with no warning, a hand jammed hard into my back and sent me crashing to the floor. I gave a yell of pain and rolled over, gazing blindly into the pitch-black depths.

"Who's there?" I asked shakily. A dry chuckle answered me. "Who is that?" I gasped. "Mr Crepsley? Is that you? Did you follow me down? Is it—"

"No," Murlough whispered in my ear. "It's not." He flicked on a torch, directly in front of my eyes.

The light was blinding. I gasped and shut my eyes, thoughts of defending myself forgotten. It was what the vampaneze had been waiting for. Before I could react, he ducked forward, opened his mouth and breathed on me ... the breath of the undead ... the gas which knocks people out.

I tried drawing back, but it was too late. The gas was in me. It raced up my nostrils and down my throat, flooding my lungs, forcing me to double over, coughing fitfully.

The last thing I remember was falling forwards, Murlough's bare purple feet growing larger as I dropped towards them.

And then ... nothing. Just black.

# CHAPTER TWENTY-ONE

WHEN I came to, I found myself face to face with a skull. Not any old skull, either — this still had flesh on it, and one of the eyeballs was floating in its socket.

I screamed and tried pulling away, but couldn't. Looking up (*up?* Why wasn't I looking *down?*) at my body, I realized I was bound tightly with ropes. After a few seconds of puzzled panic, I noticed another rope around my ankles, and it dawned on me that I was hanging upside down.

"I bet the world looks different from there, hmmm?" Murlough said. Twisting around — I couldn't move my limbs, but I could swing about — I saw him sitting a little way from the skull, chewing on a fingernail. He stuck out a foot and began rocking the skull. "Say hello to Evra," he chuckled.

"*No!*" I screamed, swinging forward, baring my teeth, trying to bite deep into his leg. Unfortunately, the rope wouldn't stretch that far. "You promised you wouldn't kill him before Christmas!" I cried.

"You mean it *isn't* Christmas?" Murlough asked innocently. "Whoops! Sorry. Bit of a boo-boo, hmmm?"

"I'll kill you," I swore. "I'm going to—"

A groan stopped me short. Turning, I noticed I wasn't alone. Somebody else was strung upside down, a couple of metres away.

"Who's that?" I asked, certain it was Mr Crepsley. "Who's there?"

"D-D-D-Darren?" a tiny voice said.

"*Evra?*" I gasped with disbelief.

Murlough laughed and flicked on a strong torch. It took my eyes a few seconds to adjust to the light. When they did, I was able to make out the familiar shape and features of the snake-boy. He looked hungry, exhausted and scared — but he was alive.

Evra was alive!

"Fooled you, didn't I?" Murlough giggled, shuffling closer.

"What are you doing here, Darren?" Evra moaned. His face was badly cut and bruised, and I could see a pinkish patch on his right arm and shoulder where scales had been brutally hacked off. "How did he—"

"That's enough out of you, reptile!" Murlough growled, kicking out at Evra, sending him snapping back on his rope.

"Stop that!" I roared.

"Make me," Murlough laughed. "Be quiet," he warned Evra. "If you speak again without permission, they'll be your last words. Understand?" Evra nodded feebly. All the fight had been hammered out of him. He was a pitiful sight. But at least he was alive. That was the main thing.

I began to take in my surroundings. We were in a large cavern. It was too dark to tell if it was natural or man-made. Evra and me were hanging from a steel bar. Skeletons littered the floor. I could hear water dripping somewhere, and spotted a rough bed in one corner.

"Why have you brought me here?" I asked.

"Snakey was lonely," Murlough answered. "I thought you'd be good company for him, hmmm?"

"How did you find me?"

"Wasn't hard," Murlough said. "Wasn't hard. Heard you and the vampire coming from miles away. Followed you. Murlough knows these pipes like the back of his teeth, yes he does. Young Murlough's smart. Been down here long enough. Wasn't just twiddling my thumbs."

"Why didn't you attack?" I asked. "I thought you wanted to kill Mr Crepsley."

"I *will*," Murlough said. "Biding my time. Waiting for the right moment. Then you stormed off and made things easy. Young Murlough couldn't pass up a gift. I'll get the vampire later. You'll do for now. You and Snakey."

"Mr Crepsley was alone," I baited him. "He had no torch. He was in the dark. But you decided to come after *me*. You're a coward. You were too scared to attack someone your own size. You're no better than—"

Murlough's fist connected with my jaw and I saw stars.

"Say that again," he hissed, "and I'll slice off an ear."

I stared at the vampaneze with loathing, but held my tongue.

"Murlough's afraid of nothing!" he told me. "Especially not a weak old vampire like Crepsley. What sort of a vampire is it that consorts with children, hmmm? He isn't worth bothering with. I'll pick him off later. You have more guts. You're more hot-blooded." Murlough bent and tweaked my cheeks. "I like hot blood," he said softly.

"You can't drink from me," I said. "I'm a half-vampire. I'm off limits."

"Perhaps I'm finished with limits. I'm a free agent. I answer to no one. The laws of the vampaneze don't trouble me down here. I'll do what I like."

"It's poison," I gasped. "Vampire blood is poison to vampaneze."

"Is it?"

"Yes. So's snake blood. You can't drink from either of us."

Murlough pulled a face. "You're right about the snake blood," he grumbled. "I took a bit from him — just testing, you understand, just testing — and threw up for hours after."

"I told you!" I said triumphantly. "We're no good to you. Our blood's worthless. It can't be drunk."

"You're right," Murlough murmured, "but it can be *shed*. I can kill and eat the two of you, even if I can't drink from you." He began pushing us, so that we were soon swinging about wildly. I felt sick.

Then Murlough went to fetch something. When he returned, he was carrying two huge knives. Evra began whimpering quietly when he saw the blades.

"Ah! Snakey remembers what these are for," Murlough laughed evilly. He sliced the knives together, producing a sharp, grating sound that made me shiver. "We had some fun with these, didn't we, reptile?"

"I'm sorry, Darren," Evra sobbed. "He made me tell him where you were. I couldn't help it. He cut my scales off and ... and..."

"It's all right," I said calmly. "It's not your fault. I would have talked too. Besides, that wasn't how he caught me. We left the hotel before he found it."

"You must have left your brains behind, too," Murlough said. "Did you really think you could waltz down here into my lair, rescue the snake-boy and trot along like a merry little lamb? Did it never occur to you that I am master of this domain, and would do all in my power to stop you?"

"It occurred to me," I said softly.

"But you came anyway?"

"Evra's my friend," I said simply. "I'd do anything to help him."

Murlough shook his head and snorted. "That's the human in you. If you were a full-vampire, you'd have known better. I'm surprised Crepsley came so far with you before bottling out."

"He didn't bottle out!" I shouted.

"Yes he did, yes he did," Murlough laughed. "I followed him to the top. That's why I didn't come after you sooner, hmmm? He ran as if the sun itself was at his back."

"You're lying," I said. "He wouldn't run. He wouldn't leave me."

"No?" The vampaneze grinned. "You don't know him as well as you think, boy. He's gone. He's out of the game. He's probably halfway back to wherever it was he came from by now, fleeing with his tail between his legs."

Murlough leapt forward without warning and swung the two knives at my face, one from either side. I screamed and shut my eyes, expecting him to draw blood. But he stopped just millimetres short of my flesh, tapped my ears with them, then drew back.

"Just testing," he said. "Wanted to see how much moral fibre you have. Not much, hmmm? Not much. Snakey didn't scream until the fourth or fifth lunge. You're going to be less fun than I thought. Maybe I won't bother torturing you. Perhaps I'll kill you outright. Would you like that, half-vampire? It would be for the best: no pain, no suffering, no nightmares. Snakey has nightmares. Tell him about your nightmares, reptile. Tell him how you jerk awake, screaming and sobbing like a baby."

Evra pulled his lips in tight and said nothing.

"Oh-ho!" Murlough smirked. "Getting brave again in front of your friend, are you? Rediscovering your courage, hmmm? Well, don't worry — we won't be long knocking it out of you."

He scraped the knives together again and circled around behind us, where we couldn't see him. "Which one shall I start with?" he mused, hopping about behind us. "I think ... I'll choose..." He went very quiet. I could feel the hairs on the back of my neck standing upright.

"*You!*" he suddenly roared, and threw himself on ... *me*.

# CHAPTER TWENTY-TWO

MURLOUGH PULLED my head back. I felt the blade of a knife poking into the soft flesh of my throat. I stiffened in anticipation of the cut. I wanted to scream, but the blade stopped me. "This is it," I thought. "This is the end. What a lousy, useless way to die."

But the vampaneze was only teasing me. He slowly removed the knife and laughed nastily. He had all the time in the world. There was no reason for him to rush. He wanted to play with us a while.

"You shouldn't have come," Evra muttered. "It was stupid." He paused. "But thanks anyway," he added.

"Would *you* have left *me*?" I asked.

"Yes," he said, but I knew he was lying.

"Don't worry," I told him. "We'll figure a way out of this yet."

"*A way out?*" Murlough boomed. "Don't talk rubbish. How are you going to escape? Chew through the ropes? You could if you could reach them with your teeth, but you can't. Snap them with your super vampire strength? No good. They're too strong. I tested them myself in advance, hmmm?

"Face it, Darren Shan — you're doomed! Nobody's going to ride to the rescue. Nobody can find you down here. I'm going to take my time, cut you up into iddy-biddy pieces, drop you all over the city — like confetti — and there isn't a thing you can do about it, so *wise up!*"

"At least let Evra go," I begged. "You've got me. You don't need him. Think how horrible it'd be for him if you let him go: he'd have to live with the knowledge that I'd died in his place. That would be a terrible burden. It would be even worse than killing him."

"Maybe," Murlough grunted. "But I'm a simple man. I like simple pleasures. It's a nice idea, but I'd rather slice him up slowly and painfully, if it's all the same to you. Fewer complications."

"Please," I sobbed. "Let him go. I'll do anything you want. I ... I ... I'll give you Mr Crepsley!"

Murlough laughed. "No go. You had the chance to do that earlier. You blew it. Besides, you couldn't lead me to him now. He's bound to have changed hotels again. Might even have fled the city."

"There must be something I can give you!" I yelled desperately. "There must be some way I can..." I stopped.

I could practically hear Murlough's ears stiffening.

"What is it?" he asked curiously after several seconds of silence. "What were you going to say?"

"Wait a minute!" I snapped. "I have to think something through." I could feel Evra's eyes on me, half-hopeful, half-resigned to the fate he felt neither of us could escape.

"Hurry up," Murlough prompted me, coming round in front of me. His purple face didn't show up well in the dim light of the cavern, so his eyes and lips appeared to be three, free-floating globs of red, while his discoloured hair looked like a strange sort of bat. "I haven't got all night," he said. "Speak while you're able."

"I was just thinking," I said quickly. "You're going to have to leave town after this, aren't you?"

"*Leave?*" Murlough bellowed. "Leave my beautiful tunnels? Never! I love it here. You know what being down here makes me feel like? As if I'm inside the body of the city. These tunnels are like veins. This cavern is the heart, where the blood of the city flows in and out." He smiled, and for once it wasn't an evil leer. "Can you imagine?" he said softly. "Living in a body, roaming the veins — the tunnels of blood — freely, as you please."

"Nevertheless," I said bluntly, "you *will* have to leave."

"What's this talk of leaving?" he snapped, jabbing me with the knife. "You're beginning to annoy me."

"I'm just being practical," I said. "You can't stay here. Mr Crepsley knows where you are. He'll return."

"That coward? I doubt it. He'll be too—"

"He'll return with *help*," I interrupted. "With other vampires."

Murlough laughed. "The Vampire Generals, do you mean?"

"Yes," I said.

"Nonsense! They can't come after me. There's an agreement between them and us. They don't interfere. Crepsley isn't a General, is he?"

"No," I said. "He's not."

"There you are!" Murlough yelled triumphantly. "He couldn't have come after me if he was. Rules and laws and ways of living. They mean as much to the vampires as they do to the vampaneze."

"All the same, the Generals *will* come," I insisted quietly. "They couldn't before, but now they can. Maybe tonight. Tomorrow for sure. Perhaps this is what Mr Crepsley intended all along."

"What are you blabbering about?" Murlough looked uneasy.

"You said something interesting a while ago," I said. "You were surprised Mr Crepsley came down here with me. I didn't think anything of it at the time, but now that I've considered it, I agree: it *was* odd of him. I thought it was because he wanted to help me find Evra, but now..."

"*What?*" Murlough screeched when I didn't go on. "Say what you're thinking. Out with it, or..." He raised the knives threateningly.

"The pact between the vampires and vampaneze," I said quickly. "It says one side can't interfere with the other, right?"

"Right," Murlough agreed.

"*Unless* it's to defend or avenge themselves."

Murlough nodded. "This is so."

I smiled weakly. "Don't you see? *I'm* a half-vampire. If you kill *me*, the Generals will have an excuse to come after you. Mr Crepsley must have planned this all along." I took a deep breath and looked Murlough straight in the eye. "He *let* you find me. He *wanted* you to grab me. He *meant* for you to kill me."

Murlough's eyes widened. "No," he wheezed. "He wouldn't."

"He's a vampire," I said. "Of course he would. This is his city. I'm just his apprentice. Which would *you* choose to sacrifice?"

"But ... but..." The vampaneze scratched his face nervously. "I didn't make the first move!" he shouted. "*You* came after *me*."

I shook my head. "*Mr Crepsley* came after you. I'm innocent. I pose no threat. If you kill me, you'll be held accountable. The Generals will descend on you, and no vampaneze will step in to defend you."

Murlough let my words sink in, in silence, then he started

jumping up and down on the spot, cursing furiously. I let him rage for a while, then I said, "It's not too late. Let me go. Let Evra go, too. Flee the city. They can't touch you then."

"But I love these tunnels," Murlough groaned.

"Do you love them enough to die for them?" I asked.

His eyes narrowed. "You're very smart, aren't you?" he snarled.

"Not really," I said. "I wouldn't have come down here if I was. But I *am* able to see the truth when it's staring me in the face. Kill me, Murlough, and you sign your own death warrant."

His shoulders sagged and I knew I was safe. Now there was only Evra to worry about...

"Snakey," Murlough said menacingly. "*He* isn't a vampire. There's nothing to stop me killing *him*, hmmm?"

"No!" I shouted. "If you harm Evra, I'll go to the Generals myself and tell them—"

"Tell them *what*?" Murlough interrupted. "Do you think they'd care? Do you think they'd risk war for the sake of a reptile?" He laughed. "Young Murlough's in a killing mood. I mightn't be able to have the little half-vampire, but I won't be cheated out of Snakey too. Watch, Darren Shan. Watch as I carve the snake-boy a new mouth – *in his belly!*"

He grabbed the ropes around Evra and tugged him forward with his left hand. With his right, he positioned one of the knives and prepared to make the first cut.

"Wait!" I screamed. "Don't do it! Don't do it!"

"Why shouldn't I?" Murlough sneered.

"I'll swap places!" I yelled. "Me for Evra."

"No good," Murlough said. "You're a half-vampire. No deal."

"I'll give you somebody else! Somebody even better!"

"Who?" Murlough laughed. "Who could you give me, Darren Shan?"

"I'll give you…" I gulped deeply, shut my eyes, and whispered the terrible words.

"What was that?" Murlough asked, pausing suspiciously. "Speak up. I didn't hear you."

"I said…" I licked my lips and forced the words out again, louder this time. "I said I'll give you my girlfriend. If you spare Evra, I'll give you … *Debbie*."

# CHAPTER TWENTY-THREE

A STUNNED silence greeted my obscene offer. Evra was the first to break it.

"No!" he screamed. "Don't do it! You can't!"

"Debbie for Evra," I said, ignoring Evra's pleas. "How about it?"

"Debbie?" Murlough scratched his cheeks slowly. It took him a few seconds to work out who I was referring to. Then he remembered and smiled. "Ah! *Debbie!* Darren Shan's tasty girlfriend." His eyes twinkled as he thought about her.

"She'd be more use to you than Evra," I said. "You could drink from her. You said you'd like to. You said she'd have nice blood."

"Yes," Murlough agreed. "Salty. Juicy." He took a step back from Evra. "But why choose?" he mused aloud. "Why not have both? Kill the snake-boy now, drink from Debbie later. She won't be hard to find. I can watch the Square tomorrow, find out where she lives, and as soon as night comes..." He grinned.

"You don't have time," I said. "You must leave the city tonight. You can't wait."

"Still yapping on about leaving?" Murlough snorted. "If I

let you go — as you've convinced me I should — I won't have to leave."

"Yes you will," I contradicted him. "It'll take a while for the vampires to discover I'm alive. The Generals will come straight down these tunnels when they arrive. They'll find out about me eventually, but if they kill you beforehand..."

"They wouldn't dare!" Murlough shrieked. "It would mean war!"

"But they wouldn't know that. They'd think they were in the right. They'd pay dearly for their mistake, but that would be no consolation as far as you're concerned. You must leave, as soon as possible. You can return in a couple of weeks, but if you stick around now, it'll be a recipe for disaster."

"Young Murlough doesn't want to leave," the vampaneze pouted. "I like it here. I don't want to go. But you're right," he sighed. "For a few nights, at least, I must get out. Find a dark abandoned cellar. Hole up. Lay low."

"That's why Debbie would be better than Evra," I pressed on. "You must be hungry. You'll want to feed before leaving, yes?"

"Oh yes," Murlough agreed, rubbing his bloated belly.

"But feeding without planning is dangerous. Vampires are used to it, but vampaneze aren't, are they?"

"No," Murlough said. "We're smarter than vampires. We think ahead. Plan it out. Mark our meals in advance."

"But you can't do that now," I reminded him. "You need a quick snack to keep you ticking over while you're away. *I* can provide that. Agree to my terms and I'll take you to Debbie. I can get you in and out without anybody knowing."

"Darren! Stop!" Evra roared. "I don't want this! You can't—"

Murlough punched Evra hard in the belly, shutting him up.

"How can I trust you?" the vampaneze hissed. "How do I know you won't trick me?"

"How could I?" I retorted. "Keep my hands bound behind my back. Keep a knife close to my throat. Leave Evra where he is — I'll come back for him later, once you've fed and left. If I try anything, I'll be dooming us both. I'm not stupid. I know what's at stake."

Murlough hummed tunelessly as he thought it over.

"You mustn't do this," Evra moaned.

"It's the only way," I said softly.

"I don't want to trade Debbie's life for mine," he said. "I'd rather die myself."

"See if you think that way tomorrow," I grunted.

"How can you do it?" he asked. "How can you give her up as if she was just a ... a..."

"A *human*," I said shortly.

"I was going to say *animal*."

I smiled thinly. "To a vampire it's the same thing. You're my best friend, Evra. Debbie's just a human I was soft on."

Evra shook his head. "I don't recognize you any longer," he said sadly, and turned away from me.

"All right," Murlough reached a decision. He drew back his knives, then thrust them forward. I winced, but he only cut the rope around my ankles. I fell heavily to the floor. "We'll do it your way," the vampaneze declared. "But if you put one foot out of place..."

"I won't," I said, getting up. "Now — how about your word?"

"What?"

"You haven't given it to me yet. I'm not leaving without it."

The vampaneze grinned. "Clever boy," he gurgled. "All right. I give you my word — the girl for Snakey. Debbie for Evra.

Is that good enough for you?"

I shook my head. "Say you'll let me go when you're finished with Debbie. Say you won't stop me coming back to free Evra. Say you'll do nothing to harm either of us afterwards."

Murlough laughed. "Oh, you're clever all right. Almost as clever as young Murlough. Very well. I'll let you go. I'll do nothing to stop you coming back, or hurt you once you're free." He raised a finger. "But if you ever return to this city, or if our paths cross in the future, it'll be death. This is a temporary reprieve, not a long-term guarantee. Agreed?"

"Agreed."

"Very well. Shall we make a start?"

"Aren't you going to undo a few of these ropes?" I asked. "I can barely walk like this."

"*Barely* is good enough," Murlough laughed. "I'm not going to take any chances with you. I've got a feeling you wouldn't miss a trick." He shoved me hard in the back. I stumbled, then found my feet and began to walk.

I glanced over my shoulder at Evra. "I won't be long," I said. "I'll be back before dawn and we'll both go home to the Cirque Du Freak, OK?"

He didn't answer. He refused to even look at me.

Sighing, I turned around and started out of the lair, Murlough guiding me through the tunnels, singing gruesome little songs as he skipped along after me, telling me what he was going to do once he got his foul hands on Debbie.

# CHAPTER TWENTY-FOUR

WE PASSED quickly through the tunnels. Murlough marked the walls as he went, scratching them with his nails. He didn't want to, but I told him the deal was off if he didn't. This way, I would only have to follow the marks when I returned. Much simpler than trying to remember every twist and turn.

Murlough had to carry me whenever crawling or climbing was required. I hated being so close to him – his breath stank of human blood – but had to put up with it. He wasn't going to loosen the ropes around my arms, no matter what the circumstances.

We left the tunnels by a drain close to the Square. Murlough hauled me up, only to yank me down sharply when a car passed nearby.

"Have to be careful," he hissed. "Police have been over the city like flies since they found the bodies. Most annoying. In future I'll bury bones more carefully."

He brushed some dirt off his white suit when he stood, but made no effort to clean mine. He tutted, annoyed. "Have to get new clothes when I come back," he said. "Very awkward. Can never visit the same tailor twice, hmmm?"

"Why not?" I asked.

He cocked an eyebrow at me. "Is this a face you would forget in a hurry?" he asked, pointing to his purplish skin and red features. "Nobody would. That's why I have to kill any tailor once he's measured and fitted me. I'd steal clothes from shops if I could, but I am of uncommon build." He patted his gross belly and giggled.

"Come," he said. "Lead on. Take the back route. Less chance of being seen."

The streets were virtually deserted – it was late on Christmas Eve, and the melting snow meant walking was a slippy business – and we met no one. We trudged through the slush, Murlough shoving me to the floor whenever a car drove by. I was getting sick of it – unable to break my fall with my hands, my face was taking the worst of the punishment – but he only laughed when I complained.

"Toughen you up, hmmm?" he said. "Build muscles."

Eventually we reached Debbie's. Murlough paused at the darkened back door and glanced around nervously. The surrounding houses were in darkness, but still he hesitated. For a moment I thought he was going to back out of our deal.

"Scared?" I asked softly.

"Young Murlough's scared of nothing!" he snapped immediately.

"Then what are you waiting for?"

"You seem very keen to lead me to your girlfriend," he said suspiciously.

I shrugged as best I could beneath the ropes. "The longer I have to wait, the worse I'm going to feel," I said. "I know what has to be done. I don't like it, and I'll feel awful afterwards, but all I want right now is to have it over and done with, so I can fetch Evra and find someplace warm to lie down and relax. My feet are like blocks of ice."

"Poor little half-vampire," Murlough giggled, then used one of his sharp vampaneze nails to cut a circle in the glass of the back door window. Reaching in, he opened the door and shoved me through.

He listened quietly to the noises of the house.

"How many people live here?" he asked.

"Three," I said. "Debbie and her parents."

"No brothers or sisters?" I shook my head. "No lodgers?"

"Just the three of them," I repeated.

"I might nibble one of the parents when I'm finished with the girl," he muttered.

"That wasn't part of the deal!" I hissed.

"So what? I never said I'd spare them. I doubt if I'll be hungry after, but maybe I'll come back another night, pick them off one by one. They'll think it's a family curse." He giggled.

"You're disgusting," I growled.

"You're only saying that because you like me," he chuckled. "Go on," he said, snapping back to serious business. "Up the stairs. The parents' bedroom first. I want to make sure they're asleep."

"Of course they're asleep," I said. "It's the middle of the night. You'd hear them if they were awake."

"I don't want them walking in on me," he said.

"Look," I sighed, "if you want to check on Jesse and Donna, fine, I'll take you to them. But you're wasting time. Wouldn't it be better if we got in and out as quickly as possible?"

The vampaneze thought it over. "Very well," he said. "But if they pop up unexpected, young Murlough will kill them, yes he will, and it'll be *your* fault."

"Fair enough," I said, and started up the stairs.

It was a long, tense walk. Being bound by ropes, I wasn't able to move as quietly as usual. Every time a step creaked, I winced and paused. Murlough was tense too: his hands were twitching and he drew in a sharp breath whenever I made a noise and stopped.

When I got to Debbie's door, I leant my head against it and sighed morosely. "This is it," I said.

"Out of the way," Murlough snapped, and shoved me to one side. He stood there, sniffing, then smiled. "Yes," he gurgled. "I can smell her blood. You can smell it too, I bet, hmmm?"

"Yes," I said.

He turned the handle and eased the door open. It was dark inside, but our eyes were used to the greater darkness of the tunnels, so they adjusted quickly.

Murlough glanced around the room, noting the wardrobes and chests of drawers, the few posters and pieces of furniture, the bare Christmas tree near the window.

Debbie's outline could just be seen beneath the covers of her bed, moving about slightly, as a person does when they're having a bad dream. The smell of her blood was thick in the air.

Murlough started forward, then remembered me. He tied me to the door handle, tugged at it hard to make sure the knot was secure, then jammed his face up to mine and sneered.

"Have you ever seen death before, Darren Shan?" he asked.

"Yes," I said.

"It's wonderful, isn't it?"

"No," I said bluntly. "It's horrible."

The vampaneze sighed. "You cannot see the beauty. Never mind. You are young. You will learn as you grow." He pinched my chin between a couple of purple fingers and a thumb. "I want you to watch," he said. "Watch as I rip her throat open. Watch as I suck her blood out. Watch as I steal her soul and make it mine."

I tried turning my eyes away but he pinched harder and forced them back. "If you don't watch," he said, "I go straight to the parents' room after this and kill the two of them too. Understand?"

"You're a monster," I gasped.

"*Understand?*" he repeated menacingly.

"Yes," I said, jerking my chin free. "I'll watch."

"Good boy," he chuckled. "Clever boy. You never know — you might like it. This could be the making of you. Perhaps you'll come with me when I leave. How about it, Darren Shan? Fancy abandoning that boring old vampire and becoming young Murlough's assistant, hmmm?"

"Just get on with it," I said, not bothering to hide my disgust.

Murlough crossed the room slowly, making no sound. He drew his two knives as he walked and twirled them about like a pair of batons. He began whistling, but softly, too softly for any but the most advanced ears to hear.

The slight movements continued beneath the covers.

I watched, stomach churning, as he closed in on his prey. Even if I hadn't been under orders to watch, I couldn't have torn my eyes away. It was a dreadful sight but fascinating. Like watching a spider zoom in on a fly. Only *this* spider carried knives, ate humans and had an entire city for a web.

He approached the bed from the side nearest the door, stopping half a metre away. Then he produced something from one of his pockets. Straining my eyes, I realized it was a bag. Opening it, he took out some kind of salt-like substance and sprinkled it on the floor. I wanted to ask what it was for, but didn't dare speak. I guessed it was some ritual that vampaneze performed when they killed somebody at home. Mr Crepsley had told me they were big on rituals.

Murlough walked around the bed, sprinkling the "salt", muttering words I could make no sense of. When he was finished, he strolled back to the foot of the bed, glanced over to make sure I was watching, and then, in one swift move — almost too quick for me to follow — leapt on the bed, landed with a foot on either side of the sleeping form, jerked back the covers and lashed out with both knives, killer cuts which would slash open Debbie's throat and end her life in an instant.

# CHAPTER TWENTY-FIVE

MURLOUGH'S KNIVES swished through air, through the space where Debbie's neck should have been, and through the soft fabric of the pillows and the mattress.

But not through Debbie.

Because Debbie wasn't there.

Murlough stared down at the creature tied to the bed, its hooves and snout bound as tightly as I was.

"It's ... a..." His jaws quivered. He couldn't bring himself to say the word.

"It's a *goat*," I finished for him, smiling grimly.

Murlough turned slowly, his face a mask of confusion. "But ... but ... but..."

While he was spluttering, trying to figure out what was happening, the door of one of the wardrobes opened and Mr Crepsley stepped out.

The vampire looked even more sinister than the vampaneze, with his blood-red clothes and cloak, his orange crop of hair and ugly scar.

Murlough froze when he saw Mr Crepsley. His red eyes bulged out of his head and his purple skin lightened a couple of shades as blood rushed from his face.

From the movies I'd seen, I was expecting a long, exciting fight. I thought the two would trade insults first, then Mr Crepsley would draw a knife or a sword and they'd lunge and parry at one another, battling their way around the room, nicking each other in the early stages, gradually working up to the more serious wounds.

But it wasn't like that. This was a fight between super-fast predators of the night who were only interested in killing, not impressing action-hungry audiences. There were just four moves in the conflict, and it was over in the space of two blurred and furious seconds.

Mr Crepsley made the first move. His right hand zipped out and sent a short knife flying through the air. It struck Murlough in the upper left of his chest, a few centimetres higher than its target — his heart. The vampaneze recoiled and drew in air to scream.

While Murlough's mouth was opening, Mr Crepsley sprang forward. One huge leap was all it took, then he was at the side of the bed, in position to go hand-to-hand with the vampaneze.

That was the second move of the fight.

The third move was Murlough's — his only one. In a panic, he lashed out at Mr Crepsley with his left-handed knife. The blade glittered through the air at a frightening speed and would have made an end of the vampire had it been on target. But it wasn't. It soared a good six centimetres above the vampire's head.

As Murlough's left arm followed through on the swing, it left a gap which Mr Crepsley exploited. Using only his bare right hand, he delivered the killer blow. Keeping the hand flat, rough nails jutting out like five sharp blades, he drove it into Murlough's belly.

And when I say into, I *mean* into!

Murlough gasped and went deathly still. The knife dropped from his hand and he gazed down. Mr Crepsley's hand had disappeared into the flesh of the vampaneze's belly, all the way up to his forearm.

He left the hand there a moment, then yanked back sharply, bringing guts and a torrent of dark blood with it.

Murlough groaned and collapsed to his knees, almost squashing the goat in the process, then toppled to the floor, where he rolled over on to his back and tried closing the hole in his belly with spit he'd quickly licked on to the palms of his hands.

But the hole was too wide. The vampaneze's healing spit was useless. There was nothing he could do to seal the flesh or stop his precious blood from pumping out. He was finished.

Mr Crepsley stepped back from the dying vampaneze, picked up one of the bedsheets and wiped his hand on it. His face was expressionless. He appeared neither pleased nor saddened by what he had done.

After a couple of seconds, Murlough realized his situation was hopeless. Flopping over on to his belly, his eyes settled on me, and he began crawling towards me, gritting his teeth against the pain.

"Mr Crepsley?" I said shakily.

Mr Crepsley studied the crawling vampaneze, then shook his head. "Do not worry. He can do you no harm." But, taking no chances, he walked over, freed me, and stood by my side, ready to strike again if needed.

It was a long, agonized crawl for the vampaneze. I almost felt sorry for him, but had only to think of Evra strung up, and what he'd planned to do to Debbie, to remind myself that he deserved everything he'd got.

He paused more than once, and I thought he was going to

die midway, but he was determined to have his final say, and fought on, even though he must have known he was hastening the moment of his death.

He collapsed on his face at my feet and breathed heavily into the carpet. Blood was gushing out of his mouth and I knew the end was almost upon him. He raised a trembling finger and crooked it, beckoning me to lean down.

I glanced questioningly at Mr Crepsley.

The vampire shrugged. "He is harmless now. It is up to you."

I decided to see what the dying vampaneze had to say. I bent down and leant close to his mouth. He had only seconds left.

His red eyes rolled directionlessly in their sockets. Then, with an immense effort, they fixed on me and his lips split into one last leer. He raised his head as high as he could and whispered something that I couldn't hear.

"I didn't catch that," I told him. "You'll have to speak up." I jammed my ear closer to his mouth.

Murlough licked his lips, clearing some blood and making space for air. Then, with his final breath, he got out the words that seemed so important to him.

"Cluh-cluh-clever buh-buh-buh-boy, hmmm?" he gurgled, then smiled blankly and fell forward.

He was dead.

# CHAPTER TWENTY-SIX

WE BUNDLED Murlough's body into a large black plastic bag. We'd drop him off later in the tunnels of blood he'd loved so much. As fitting a burial place as any for him.

We stuck the goat in a bag too, but made a couple of air holes in it. We'd expected Murlough to kill the goat, which I'd stolen earlier from the children's section of the city zoo. Mr Crepsley wanted to take it back to the Cirque Du Freak — it would provide a nice snack for Evra's snake or the Little People — but I persuaded him to set it free.

Next we cleaned up the mess. Murlough had shed a lot of blood, all of which had to be mopped up. We didn't want the Hemlocks to find it and start asking questions. We worked quickly but it took a couple of hours.

With the cleaning finished, we climbed up to the attic and brought down the sleeping bodies of Jesse, Donna and Debbie, and laid them in their respective beds.

The entire night had been planned. The wine I brought for dinner? I drugged it when I was in the kitchen. I added one of Mr Crepsley's potions to the wine, a tasteless little concoction that knocked everybody out within ten minutes.

They'd be asleep for several more hours yet, and wake with sore heads, but otherwise no ill-effects.

I smiled as I wondered what they'd think when they woke in bed, fully dressed, with no memories of the previous night. It would be a mystery, one they'd never solve.

It hadn't been a perfect plan. Lots of things could have gone wrong. For starters, there was no guarantee that Murlough would find me when I had my "fight" with Mr Crepsley and stormed off on my own, and no guarantee that he wouldn't kill me straightaway if he did.

He could have gagged me when he caught me, in which case I would have been unable to convince him that he ought to let me live. Or he might have disregarded my warning about the Vampire Generals — what I said was true, but the trouble was, Murlough was mad. There was no telling how a mad vampaneze would act. He might have laughed at the threat of the Generals and sliced me up anyway.

Convincing him to swap Evra for Debbie was always going to be the trickiest bit. For it to work, I'd had to deliver a perfect performance. If I'd come straight out and made the offer, Murlough might have been suspicious and not walked into the trap. If he'd been in full control of his senses, I don't think he *would* have fallen for it, regardless of my performance, so on that score his madness worked in our favour.

And, of course, there was the killing of him to account for. Murlough *could* have beaten Mr Crepsley. If he had, all six of us would have died: Mr Crepsley, me and Evra, Debbie, Donna and Jesse.

It had been a dangerous gamble — and unfair to the Hemlocks, who knew nothing of their role in the deadly game — but sometimes you've got to take chances. Was it wise to risk five lives for the sake of one? Probably not. But it was *human*. If I'd learned nothing else from my encounter with the mad vampaneze it was that even the undead could be human. We *had* to be — without a touch of humanity, we'd be like Murlough, nothing more than bloodthirsty monsters of the night.

I tucked Debbie in under the fresh covers. There was a tiny scar near her left ankle, where Mr Crepsley had drawn blood earlier. He'd needed the blood to smear on the goat, in order to mislead Murlough's sense of smell.

I looked up at the vampire. "You did well tonight," I said quietly. "Thanks."

He smiled. "I did what had to be done. It was *your* plan. I should be the one offering the thanks, were it not for the fact that you got in the way when I first had him in my sights. In my eyes, that makes us even, so neither need thank the other."

"What will happen when the vampaneze find out we killed him?" I asked. "Will they come after us?"

Mr Crepsley sighed. "With luck, they will not find the body. If they do, they will hopefully be unable to trace him to us."

"But if they do?" I pressed him for an answer.

"Then they will hunt us to the ends of the Earth," he said. "And they will kill us. We would not stand a chance. They would come in their dozens and the Generals would not assist us."

"Oh," I said. "I wish I hadn't asked."

"Would you rather I'd lied?"

I shook my head. "No. No more lies." I smiled. "But I think it'll be for the best if we don't tell Evra. What he doesn't know can't worry him. Besides, he's mad enough at me as it is. He thought I was really going to trade Debbie's life for his. He's furious."

"He will calm down when the facts are explained," Mr Crepsley said confidently. "Now — shall we go and collect him?"

I hesitated and glanced down at Debbie. "Can I have a couple of minutes to myself?" I asked.

"Of course," Mr Crepsley said. "But do not delay: dawn approaches and I do not wish to spend tomorrow trapped in those godforsaken tunnels. I will be downstairs." He departed.

I checked my watch. Nearly four in the morning. That meant this was the twenty-fifth of December. Christmas Day.

I worked quickly. I placed the bare Christmas tree to one side of Debbie's bed, opened the box of decorations and covered the tree with glittering balls, tiny figures, streams of tinsel and twinkling lights. When I had finished, I turned Debbie so that she was facing towards the tree. It would be the first thing she'd see when she opened her eyes in the morning.

I felt bad about leaving without saying goodbye. This way, I hoped to make it up to her. When she woke and saw the tree, she'd know I hadn't slipped away thoughtlessly. She'd know I'd been thinking of her, and hopefully wouldn't hold my sudden disappearance against me.

I stood over her a few seconds, studying her face. This would almost certainly be the last time I'd ever see her. She looked so sweet, lying there asleep. I was tempted to find a camera and take a photo, but I didn't need to — this was one picture I'd always be able to remember in perfect detail. It would join those of my parents, my sister, Sam — cherished faces which would never fade in the mental galleries of my memory.

Leaning forward, I kissed her forehead and brushed a

stray lock of hair out of her eyes. "Merry Christmas, Debbie," I said softly, then turned and left, and went to rescue Evra.

**TO BE CONTINUED…**

# VAMPIRE MOUNTAIN

THE BEAR meant to kill me — there was no doubt about that — and it would have, if not for the wolf cub, who leapt courageously from the tree. It landed on top of the bear's head, momentarily blinding it.

The bear roared and swiped at it with a huge paw. The cub bit one of its ears, and the bear roared again, this time with pain. Then, shaking its head viciously from side to side, it sent the cub flying into a nearby thicket.

The bear resumed its attack on me once it had disposed of the wolf cub, but in the time the cub had bought, I'd ducked round the tree and was running for the cave as fast as I could. The bear lurched after me, realized I was too fast for it, bellowed angrily, then turned on the young wolf once more.

I stopped when I heard the cub's frightened yapping. Glancing over my shoulder, I saw the cub had made it back up the tree, the bark of which the bear was now ripping to pieces with its claws in an attempt to reach him. Although the cub was in no immediate danger, I knew that sooner or later he'd slip or the bear would shake him down, and that would be the end of him.

I paused no more than a second, deciding whether to run ahead to the safety of the cave, or go back and risk my life trying to save the cub. Then I turned, picked up a rock and the thickest stick I could find, and sped back.

The bear let go of the tree when it saw me coming, dropped to its haunches and prepared to meet my challenge. It was a burly beast, maybe a metre and a half high, black fur, a white quarter-moon mark spread across its chest, and a whitish face. Foam flecked its jaws and its eyes were wild, as though touched by madness. Maybe it had rabies!

I stopped several metres in front of the bear and whacked the ground with my stick. The bear snarled and advanced. I glanced up at the cub, hoping he'd have enough sense to slink down the tree and scamper to the cave, but he stayed where he was.

The bear swiped at me but I ducked easily out of the way of its massive paw. Rearing up on its hind legs, it fell upon me, hoping to crush me with the weight of its huge body. I avoided the beast again but it was a closer call this time. I knew that if this went on much longer, it would make contact in the end — fatal contact.

I was thrusting the end of the stick at the bear's face, aiming at its eyes, when the two she-wolves rushed on to the scene and threw themselves at the beast. They must have heard the cub's yapping and come to investigate.

The bear howled as one of the wolves bit deep in to its shoulder, while the other attached herself to its rear legs, tearing at them with her teeth and claws. The bear shook off one wolf and bent to deal with the other, and at that moment I darted in with my stick and jabbed at its left ear.

I must have hurt the beast, because it lost interest in the wolves and hurled itself at me once again. I ducked out of the way of its body but one of its massive forelegs connected with the side of my head and I fell to the ground, dazed.

The bear rolled to its feet and made for me, scattering the wolves with quick swipes. I scrabbled backwards, but not fast enough. Suddenly, the bear was above me, it's crescent-shaped mark looking oddly similar to the moon that was shining overhead.

It reared up on it's hind legs again, bellowing triumphantly.

It had me exactly where it wanted. I slammed the stick against its stomach, then hurled the rock at it, but the bear took no notice of such feeble blows. Leering, it started to fall…

…which was when the two Little People barrelled into its back and knocked it off balance. They must have followed the wolves and their timing couldn't have been sweeter as far as I was concerned.

The bear must have thought the entire world was conspiring against it. Every time it had me in its sights, something new got in the way. Roaring as loud as it could at the Little People, it charged at them wildly. The one with the limp stepped out of its way but the other got trapped beneath it.

The Little Person raised his short arms and jammed them against the bear's torso, trying to shove it to one side. He was strong, and for a second I thought he would succeed. But not even a vampire would have stood a chance against such a massive foe, and the bear came crashing down on top of the Little Person, driving him to the ground.

There was a horrible crunching sound and as the bear got to its feet, I saw the Little Person lying in pieces, all bloody and broken, with bones jutting out of its body – he looked like a squashed porcupine.

The huge animal lifted its head and bellowed ferociously at the sky, then fixed its hungry eyes on me. Dropping on all fours, the bear advanced…

# DARREN SHAN
## CIRQUE DU FREAK

**THE SAGA OF DARREN SHAN**
**BOOK 1**

Darren Shan is just an ordinary schoolboy – until he gets an invitation to visit the Cirque Du Freak… until he meets Madam Octa… until he comes face to face with a creature of the night.

Soon, Darren and his friend Steve are caught in a deadly trap. Darren must make a bargain with the one person who can save Steve. But that person is not human and only deals in blood…

ISBN 978 0 00 675416 9

www.darrenshan.com

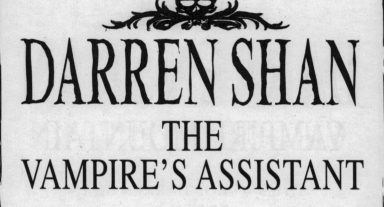

# DARREN SHAN

# THE VAMPIRE'S ASSISTANT

## THE SAGA OF DARREN SHAN
## BOOK 2

Darren Shan was just an ordinary schoolboy – until his visit to the Cirque Du Freak. Now, as he struggles with his new life as a Vampire's Assistant, he tries desperately to resist the one thing that can keep him alive… blood. But a gruesome encounter with the Wolf Man may change all that…

ISBN 978 0 00 675513 5

www.darrenshan.com

# DARREN SHAN
## VAMPIRE MOUNTAIN

### THE SAGA OF DARREN SHAN
BOOK 4

Darren Shan and Mr Crepsley embark on a dangerous trek to the very heart of the vampire world. But they face morethan the cold on Vampire Mountain — the vampaneeze have been there before them...

Will a meeting with the Vampire Princes restore Darren's human side, or turn him further towards the darkness? Only one thing is certain — Darren's initiation into the vampire clan is more deadly than he can ever have imagined.

ISBN 978 0 00 711441 2

www.darrenshan.com

# DARREN SHAN
## TRIALS OF DEATH

### THE SAGA OF DARREN SHAN
### BOOK 5

The Trials: seventeen ways to die unless the luck of
the vampires is with you. Darren Shan must pass five
fearsome Trials to prove himself to the vampire clan —
or face the stakes in the Hall of Death.

But Vampire Mountain holds hidden threats.
Sinister, potent forces are gathering in the darkness.
In this nightmare world of bloodshed and betrayal,
death may be a blessing...

ISBN 978 0 00 711440 5

www.darrenshan.com

# DARREN SHAN
# THE VAMPIRE PRINCE

## THE SAGA OF DARREN SHAN
### BOOK 6

Branded a traitor, betrayed by a friend, hunted by the
vampire clan – Darren Shan, the Vampire's Assistant,
faces certain death.

Can Darren reverse the odds and outwit a Vampire
Prince, or is this the end of thousands of years of
vampire rule...?

ISBN 978 0 00 711516 7

www.darrenshan.com

# DARREN SHAN
## HUNTERS OF THE DUSK

**THE SAGA OF DARREN SHAN**
**BOOK 7**

Darren Shan, The Vampire Prince, leaves Vampire Mountain on a life or death mission.

As part of an elite force, Darren scours the world in search of the Vampaneze Lord. But the road ahead is long and dangerous — and lined with the bodies of the damned...

ISBN 978 0 00 713779 4

www.darrenshan.com